Private Scho[illegible]

"Come on, Roy. You know [illegible] ...lings are going to be hurt if you don't say by[illegible]...ye." The woman was laughing. And the guy—Roy—started to laugh too.

"Okay, okay. Bye, Missy. You're a good dog. Yes, you are. Bye, Dad. Bye, Mom. In case you miss me, like, half as much as the dog does."

Roy's face froze on the screen. The voice of our ATAC contact began to speak. *"Three weeks after this video was taken, Roy Duffy left the Eagle River Academy. Dead."*

Joe let out a long, low whistle of disbelief.

I wanted to say something. But the words wouldn't come. So I just watched as Roy's face dissolved and was replaced with a still shot of a tombstone that read: "Roy Duffy. Beloved son." Followed by a set of dates that showed he'd been only fourteen when he died.

"No one disputes that Roy had a heart attack," our ATAC contact continued. *"But his parents believe that Roy had the heart attack because he was pushed beyond human endurance at a hazing ritual. The administration of the Eagle River Academy insists that hazing at the school is a thing of the past—and has been for almost a decade. Your mission is to discover the truth about hazing at the academy. You will find out the whole truth about Roy Duffy's death."*

UNDERCOVER BROTHERS™

#1 *Extreme Danger*
#2 *Running on Fumes*
#3 *Boardwalk Bust*
#4 *Thrill Ride*
#5 *Rocky Road*
#6 *Burned*
#7 *Operation: Survival*
#8 *Top Ten Ways to Die*
#9 *Martial Law*
#10 *Blown Away*
#11 *Hurricane Joe*
#12 *Trouble in Paradise*
#13 *The Mummy's Curse*
#14 *Hazed*

Available from Simon & Schuster

#14 Hazed

FRANKLIN W. DIXON

Aladdin Paperbacks
New York London Toronto Sydney

ALADDIN PAPERBACKS
An imprint of Simon & Schuster
Children's Publishing Division
1230 Avenue of the Americas,
New York, NY 10020

Designed by Lisa Vega
The text of this book was set in font Aldine 401BT.
Manufactured in the United States of America
First Aladdin Paperbacks edition February 2007
10 9 8 7 6

Library of Congress Control Number 2006929869
ISBN-13: 978-1-4169-1803-5
ISBN-10: 1-4169-1803-5
0310 - Offset Paperback Manufacturers, Dallas, PA

TABLE OF CONTENTS

JOE

1.

Hazard Flag

"Welcome to the Wild Horses Rally. We have twenty-two drivers out here today, all between the ages of thirteen and nineteen. All ready to ride the asphalt of the Philly Speedway," the announcer boomed out. "Can we give them a yee-haw?"

The crowd gave a *yee-haw* as I climbed into my Formula racer's plastic seat. It put me about four inches off the ground. I strapped myself into my safety harness and pulled on my helmet.

I was going to rule this race. It was all I was going to think about for the next sixty laps.

Then I'd get back to thinking about who had built the bomb. The bomb designed to blow when the racer it was attached to reached 175 miles per hour. And what racer in a Formula car didn't reach that speed during a race?

My brother Frank and I had found the bomb before whoever the bomber was had a chance to attach it—to whatever car was the target. We had a lot more work to do on this ATAC mission. But right now, it was time to drive.

I locked my eyes on the signal flags, waiting for my green.

"Joe," Frank's voice crackled over my headset.

I got green. And I was outta there.

"You're going down, bro," I answered. "Don't expect any mercy because we're related. I'm going to win this puppy! And that ten thousand smackeroos. And the adoration of—"

"Joe, we've got trouble," Frank interrupted.

"Can we talk about it in twenty laps?" I asked, twisting the wheel back and forth to keep control of my car. My arms—Forget my arms. My whole body was vibrating from the power of the engine. And the wind was slamming by me. No windshields in a racer.

"There's a bomb on Jenni Fisher's car. I spotted it just before the green flag went down. I didn't have any time to warn her."

"But we destroyed the bomb we found."

"There must have been a backup. If Jenni's car

hits one seventy-five, it's gonna blow," Frank answered.

I locked my eyes on Jenni's poison green racer. How fast was it going already?

"We've got to find a way to keep her speed down until the race ends," Frank answered. "I'm going to try and pull up ahead of her. Then I'll slow down."

"I'll move up on her side. That way, she won't be able to pull around and pass you," I answered. Frank and I would both get warning flags thrown at us. But that didn't matter. Nothing mattered anymore, except keeping Jenni's speed in control until the Wild Horses Rally was done.

I scanned the cars ahead of me, trying to figure out a path that would take me up by Jenni. There were eight racers between us, including Frank.

"It's not working," Frank said over my headset. "I'm trying to pass her now, and she's picking up speed to stop me. We're at about one sixty-seven already. If Jenni picks up another eight mph, she's going to blow. I'm backing off."

Up ahead, I saw Frank's orange racer drop back. But another racer in a purple car was already moving up to take his place.

"What if I try to get a hazard flag thrown?" I asked. "That would force everybody on the track to slow down."

"Yeah, but you'd have to crash," Frank told me.

"Yeah. But Jenni is going to die if we don't do something."

There was a grassy apron ringing the inside of the track. If I took the next turn a little too tight, that's all it would take. At this speed, I'd go spinning across the center—and probably right into the outside retaining wall.

The upside? A yellow flag would definitely go up, and Jenni's car would be forced to slow down. Then Frank could put on the speed—even though it was completely against the rules—and get his car in front of hers. From there he'd at least have a shot at controlling her speed.

The downside?

Were you listening to the part where I'd go crashing into the outside retaining wall?

The purple car was gaining on Jenni's green racer. She was going to have to put on speed to keep it from cutting in front of her. And she'd do it. Who wouldn't?

The turn was coming up. When I got to the apex, I turned the wheel just a little bit too hard. My tires slid below the white line.

"Don't do it, Joe!" Frank yelled.

Too late. My tires touched grass. And that was all

it took. I was shooting sideways across the middle of the track.

I couldn't see if the yellow hazard got thrown. I couldn't see anything. My world was all blurry motion as the racer spun, skidded, and then—

Slammed.

Right into the wall. At least the other racers had seen me coming and managed to get out of the way.

I struggled to get out of my harness and leaped out of the car. My engine was starting to spark flames.

I didn't care about that. My pit crew was already on the way with fire extinguishers.

I checked the flags. Yellow. Yes!

It didn't look like the racers were going more slowly. Not as they whipped past me, blasting hot air in my face. But I knew they had taken their speed down. That's what you do when you get the hazard flag. And the drivers have to hold their positions. No driver is allowed to pass another car.

I grinned when I saw Frank speed up and pass Jenni's racer. My brother lives to follow the rules. It was probably killing him.

Then he slowed down.

And slowed down.

And slowed down.

If the roar of all those engines wasn't blasting out my eardrums, I know I would have heard the crowd booing their heads off.

A black flag went up. A black flag with the number of Frank's racer on it. He was being ordered back to the pit. You only get that flag if your car has serious damage. Or if you've broken some major regulation.

Guess what Frank's flag was for?

But he just slowed down some more.

Then he stopped.

The red flag went up. That meant the officials had ended the race. All the cars were required to slow down, get into the pit lane, and get off the track.

We did it. We'd saved Jenni's life.

First time I was ever happy about losing a race.

FRANK

2.

The Mission

“How was the defensive driving class?” Aunt Trudy asked. “Did they tell you how to deal with those people who cut in front of you without signaling? Those people shouldn’t be allowed on the road, in my opinion. How many accidents do you think they cause in a year? And speeders. Does anyone even know what those numbers posted on the side of the road are?”

“Actually, Aunt Trudy, going too slow can be as dangerous as going too fast,” Joe told her. “That was one of the problems they identified for Frank. He drives like a turtle.”

“Well, Joe crashed into a wall,” I answered as I took a bite of Salisbury steak.

"What?" Mom exclaimed.

"It was a simulator," I added quickly. "A race car simulator. They let us see how it would feel to take a Formula car around a track. Since it was Formula One drivers leading the defensive driving class."

"Even so. You ran into a wall, Joe?" Mom asked my brother. "How could you possibly have run into a wall? Walls are, well—they're very large."

Joe made a choking sound but managed to swallow the rest of his food.

"Simulators. That's a good idea," my dad said. "I don't think either of you are quite ready for the real thing."

Dad knew we hadn't been at a defensive driving class. He knew we'd been on an ATAC mission. That's because he was the man who founded American Teens Against Crime. Our father is a retired cop. Retired in that way where everyone still on the force continues to ask his advice. He'd realized there were some situations where teens were the only effective undercover agents. Like the Wild Horses race. Because of the rules, only someone under twenty could have gotten out on the track as a driver and saved Jenni. Cases like these are the reason he'd created ATAC.

"The race car drivers who taught the class were concerned about teens behind the wheel," I answered.

"There's a high percentage of accidents for teenage drivers. But I think we showed them that all teenagers aren't irresponsible. A lot of us know what we're doing."

I wanted to remind Dad that we had caught the bomber. Attempted bomber. After we'd gotten Jenni off the track, we'd figured out that it was her mechanic, a former Formula One racer himself, who'd sabotaged her car.

"I'd like to send those drivers who taught you a batch of my raspberry brownies," Aunt Trudy said. "I'll start baking to—"

She was interrupted by the doorbell.

"I'll get it!" Joe jumped to his feet.

"Were you expecting someone?" Dad asked.

"Well, I never know when one of my ladies is going to drop by," Joe answered.

Dad rolled his eyes.

Joe returned to the dining room about thirty seconds later. He balanced a pizza on one hand. "Frank, help me serve this up."

"You ordered pizza?" Aunt Trudy demanded. "We haven't even finished dinner."

"It's for dessert," Joe told her. "In some countries, they always have cheese for dessert. Right, Mom?"

Our mother is a research librarian. She knows

almost everything about almost everything. What she doesn't know, she knows where to look up. "You're thinking of a cheese tray, which is sometimes served after the main meal," she answered. "It's a selection of cheeses, with perhaps some fruit. A few apple slices. Some strawberries. It isn't served hot on pizza dough."

Joe grinned. "That's why this version is so much better." He continued on to the kitchen. I followed him.

"Special delivery from Vijay, I'm assuming," I said as Joe opened the lid of the cardboard box. Vijay Patel was with ATAC too. He wanted to become a field agent like me and Joe. He'd done some mystery solving back in Calcutta before he moved to the States when he was twelve. I was pushing for ATAC to give him a shot, but right now, he worked on the intel side.

"Yep." Joe grabbed some plates out of the cupboard. I slid a slice onto each of them—revealing the video game cartridge that had been hidden under the pizza. The cartridge was labeled HAZED.

Joe picked it up and licked a glob of tomato sauce off the top. "Our next assignment tastes great," he told me.

"Let's get it upstairs and pop it in your player," I answered. My heart rate had picked up a little. It always did when Joe and I got one of the game cartridges that held the details of an ATAC job.

"We have to serve dessert first." Joe shoved the cartridge in the front pocket of his hoodie and grabbed two plates of pizza. I grabbed the folder that had come with the cartridge and shoved it under my T-shirt. Then I picked up the pizza box and another plate of pizza and followed him into the dining room.

"Madame. Monsieur," Joe said, setting plates in front of Mom and Dad. "Le Tray de Cheese."

"Aunt T, your pizza pie," I said, as I served Aunt Trudy.

"I still think it's ridiculous to eat pizza after dinner," Trudy answered. But she already had the slice halfway up to her mouth.

"Joe and I are going to eat ours upstairs. We need to get some homework done," I said.

Aunt Trudy frowned and warned us about getting crumbs on the floor, but let us leave. She didn't stop us.

Mission accomplished.

Two minutes later Joe and I were in his room. I locked my eyes on the small screen of his portable game player as Joe slid the cartridge in place.

The screen stayed black.

"Do you think it's defective?" I asked.

"Maybe. Wait, I see something," Joe answered.

The camera seemed to be moving through the darkness. Suddenly, red letters appeared. Dripping red letters written on a gray stone wall:

In the cellar, no one can hear you scream.

"Is that blood, do you think?" Joe ran his finger over the words.

"Paint. Probably paint," I said. It was hard to make a call from the image on the screen.

The camera moved away from the wall and over to a set of rough stone steps. Hooded, black-robed figures marched down the stairs. They herded a smaller group of white-robed figures, also wearing hoods.

"On your knees, maggots!" someone in the cellar commanded. It was impossible to tell who with everyone wearing hoods.

All the white-robed figures immediately dropped to the ground in front of the warning painted on the wall.

"I didn't think maggots had knees," Joe joked. But he sounded a little freaked.

I was feeling a little freaked myself. Because now I could see that all the people in white had their hands tied behind their backs. "You think ATAC sent us a horror movie by mistake?" I asked.

Before Joe could answer, the scene on the screen

changed. I'm talking 180 degrees. Now we were looking at some teenage guys playing Frisbee on a lawn so green it looked fake. A couple of them wore Eagle River Academy sweatshirts. A large colonial-style building rose up behind them.

Another quick cut, and the cellar was back on screen. And the teenage boys in white were screaming. Maybe no one outside the cellar could hear them. But they were screaming. Their hoods were thrown back and their faces were streaked with blood and grime and sweat.

Another 180. Joe and I were looking at a bunch of guys in prep school uniforms sitting in a classroom, listening intently to their teacher lecturing about Manifest Destiny.

"Are those the same guys?" Joe asked.

"I can't tell yet," I answered. The majority of the guys in the cellar still had hoods on. And the faces of the other guys were so splotched with blood it was hard to get a good look at them.

We watched in silence as a few more scenes flashed by. Boys singing in a choir. Boys doing push-ups with weights strapped to their backs. Boys rowing on a lake. Boys eating what looked like some kind of intestines.

I was expecting another TV-commercial-perfect scene of life at the academy to come next. Instead, what was clearly a home video began to play. A guy with messy brown hair in what looked like a brand-new Eagle River Academy T-shirt was holding one hand up to block the camera. "Mom, enough," he begged. "You have enough hours of tape to watch until I'm home for winter break."

"Just say good-bye to Missy," a woman's voice urged.

The guy rolled his eyes. "I'm not saying good-bye to the dog, Mom. She's a dog. She doesn't speak English. And she doesn't watch videos. 'Cause, oh, yeah, she's a dog."

"Come on, Roy. You know Missy's feelings are going to be hurt if you don't say bye-bye." The woman was laughing. And the guy—Roy—started to laugh too.

"Okay, okay. Bye, Missy. You're a good dog. Yes, you are. Bye, Dad. Bye, Mom. In case you miss me, like, half as much as the dog does."

Roy's face froze on the screen. The voice of our ATAC contact began to speak. *"Three weeks after this video was taken, Roy Duffy left the Eagle River Academy. Dead."*

Joe let out a long, low whistle of disbelief.

I wanted to say something. But the words wouldn't come. So I just watched as Roy's face dissolved and was replaced with a still shot of a tombstone that read: "Roy Duffy. Beloved son." Followed by a set of dates that showed he'd been only fourteen when he died.

"No one disputes that Roy had a heart attack," our ATAC contact continued. *"But his parents believe that Roy had the heart attack because he was pushed beyond human endurance at a hazing ritual. The administration of the Eagle River Academy insists that hazing at the school is a thing of the past—and has been for almost a decade. Your mission is to discover the truth about hazing at the academy. You will find out the whole truth about Roy Duffy's death."*

"And I thought it was going to be something like finding out if there was cheating going on at the academy Frisbee games," Joe said. Joe has this problem with joking around at inappropriate times. I think it's a younger brother thing.

"This mission, like every other mission, is top secret," the ATAC instructions continued. *"In five seconds the cartridge will be reformatted into a regular CD."*

Five seconds later the *American Idol* theme music began to play. Joe quickly clicked the game player off. "That guy Roy seemed pretty cool."

"Yeah," I agreed. "And if somebody made him have a heart attack, we're going to find out. We're not going to let anyone else die."

3.

Welcome to the Eagle River Academy

There was a double knock on my door. I didn't need to be with ATAC to know who it was. "Come on in, Dad," I called.

Dad came into the room and carefully shut the door behind him. Then he perched on the edge of my desk. "How was the 'pizza'?" he asked.

Translation: *What is your latest mission?*

"Same pizza you had downstairs," I told him.

"It's extremely likely that our half tasted the same as yours," Frank agreed.

Dad just gave us a Dad kind of look.

"We're going to be investigating whether or not there's hazing going on at a prep school," I volunteered. It's not like Dad couldn't find that out with no problem if he really wanted to. One phone call would get him every detail. "A guy might have died while he was being hazed. Or he might have had a heart attack."

Frank flipped open the folder that Vijay had delivered along with the cartridge. "Our cover is going to be that we're part of a short exchange program between the Eagle River Academy and Bayport High," he told me and Dad. "You're going to have two Eagle River students staying with you—Andrew Peterson and Jamie Chu. We need to tell Mom and Aunt Trudy about that."

"Hazing is serious stuff," Dad said. "I read an article about a week or so ago about a boy who died from water poisoning during a hazing."

"Water, not alcohol?" Frank asked.

"Binge-drinking water, especially combined with strenuous exercise—and exercise is usually a part of hazing—dilutes the sodium content of the blood," Dad explained. "Extremely low sodium levels can cause the brain to swell, and that can lead to a fatal coma."

"Whoa," I said. "I didn't think you could drink too much water."

"The boys at the fraternity didn't think so either. They thought they were being safer by not making their pledges drink alcohol. But one of the pledges still ended up dead." Dad looked from me to Frank, his face serious. "I expect you two to look out for each other. I don't want either of you getting into a potential hazing situation alone. And if you have to break cover to get out of a dangerous situation, do it."

"Dad, there's no way we'll have to break cover. We—," I began. Then Frank grabbed a pinch of skin on my wrist—out of our father's sight—and twisted it. Hard. So I shut up.

"I won't let Junior do anything stupid," Frank promised.

Junior. Junior?! Frank wasn't that much older than I was.

I jerked my hand away from Frank. "And I'll make sure to be around if *Senior* loses his walker," I said.

You know how sometimes things sound funnier in your head?

"Loser, loser, loser," our parrot, Playback, commented from his perch. He ruffled his bright-colored feathers.

"You poop on newspaper, and you call me a loser?" I muttered.

Dad stood up. "Just watch each other's backs when you're at the academy."

"We will," I promised him. "We always do."

• • • •

"I was impressed by the statistics Dean McCormack told us about the academy," Mom said as we pulled up in front of the dorm where Frank and I would be living for the next two weeks. "I don't know of another prep school that gets so many of its students into Ivy League colleges."

"But you forgot to ask about the important stuff," I told her. "Does the cafeteria have a soft ice-cream machine? If no girls go here, where do the cheerleaders come from?"

Aunt Trudy made her disapproving sound. It's kind of a cross between a goose honk and a cough. I've tried many times to imitate it but have never gotten it completely right.

Mom smiled at me. "I'll do some research and e-mail you tonight," she promised as we all climbed out of the car.

Frank and I grabbed our backpacks and gym bags out of the trunk. We lugged them into the dorm, with Mom, Dad, and Aunt T trailing behind us. There was a living-room-type setup to the left. A couple of couches, a bunch of chairs, and a huge TV. Plus a pool table.

Nice.

Straight ahead was a counter. Behind it stood a guy with military-short blond hair sorting mail into a bunch of cubbyholes. "Hey, you must be the Hardys," he called. "I'm Douglas Stillson. I'll be your tour guide. But first, we have to get your parents their new kids—for the next two weeks."

He picked up the phone behind the desk and punched in a few numbers. "Andrew, I need you and Jamie down here," he said, then hung up. "Drop your stuff over by the couch," Douglas told me and Frank. "One of the guys will bring it up for you."

"We can take it," Frank said.

"No worries. Just leave it," Douglas told us.

Frank and I dumped our gear behind the couch. That TV had to be sixty inches. This assignment might just turn out to be sweet.

"I find it somewhat hard to believe you boys in the dorm get much studying done with a television that size around," Aunt Trudy commented. It's like she can read my mind sometimes. It's frightening.

"No first-year students get to use the lounge," Douglas answered. "And no one whose grade point average falls below a B."

"Sounds reasonable," Dad said. Aunt Trudy gave the honk 'n' cough. Clearly, it didn't sound reasonable to her—though I'm not sure why, since she was a stickler about grades.

I wondered if Frank and I counted as first-year

students. It's not like we were freshmen at our school. But we'd never been here before, so . . .

"Here come Jamie and Andrew," Douglas announced. Two guys, a little younger than me, headed down the stairs. "Guys, meet the Hardys. They'll be your host family for the next two weeks."

"It's nice to meet you," my mom said. "We hope you'll have a great time while you're staying with us."

"We have a parrot," Aunt Trudy added. Aunt Trudy used to hate Playback because he was so messy. But the bird somehow won her over. Now she's like his PR agent or something.

"A parrot. That's cool," Jamie said. But I could tell he was just being polite.

"Any advice for us about Bayport High?" Andrew asked, shoving his brown hair out of his face. "It will be my third high school in less than a year. I just transferred to the academy from my school in Iowa."

"Brian Conrad is a dillweed," I volunteered. "You'll be happier if you stay away from him."

Mom almost gave Aunt Trudy's honk 'n' cough at that.

"Sorry," I mumbled. "What I meant was, Brian Conrad isn't the nicest boy in school."

"You'll be in some classes with our friend Chet. He knows you're coming and will show you around," Frank added. We'd downloaded Chet with the info before we'd left.

Andrew nodded his head. "Thanks."

"You have any advice for us?" I asked.

"Yeah, is there anyone we should stay away from?" Frank said.

Good question. I wanted to hear the answer. It could give us our first clue into figuring out the entire truth about how Roy Duffy died.

Andrew and Jamie both shot looks at Douglas. Like they wanted him to answer for them.

And he did, with no hesitation. "There's no one you have to worry about at Royce Hall," Douglas told us. "A great bunch of guys live here." He turned to Jamie and Andrew. "Let's get your stuff loaded in the car."

"We're right out front," Dad said. He led the way outside and popped the trunk of the car. Andrew and Jamie had their gear stowed in less than thirty seconds.

"So we'll see you two in a couple of weeks." Mom gave me a hard hug. Then she hugged Frank. Aunt Trudy got on the hug train too. I wondered how many guys in our new dorm were watching this good-bye party.

"Let us know if there's anything you need," Dad instructed. I knew he was thinking of backup—not my favorite pillow or a new toothbrush.

"We've got it covered," Frank answered.

Our parents climbed in the front seat. The guys got in the back. Aunt Trudy hesitated.

"Do you want me to say good-bye to Playback for you?" she asked.

"Aw. Are you worried that Playback's feelings will be hurt?" I replied. I tell you, since Aunt Trudy has gotten over thinking of Playback as a messy house on wings, she sometimes acts like he's her favorite member of the family.

"You should definitely say bye to him for us," Frank said. "And tell him he's a good bird."

Suddenly it was like I was watching the ATAC cartridge again. The part where Roy Duffy was saying good-bye to his dog to make his mom happy. It gave me the wiggins.

"You don't have to tell Playback anything. We're going to be back in two weeks," I said quickly, trying to shake off the creepy feeling.

Aunt Trudy gave me a nod as she got in the car. I shut the door for her and waved as they pulled away from the curb.

"How about a quick tour of the school?" Douglas asked me and Frank.

"Definitely," Frank said.

"Follow me. This is the shortest way to the center of the campus." Douglas walked us away from the dorm and down a sloping hill. At the bottom we hit a gravel path and followed it through some trees.

"This is the back entrance to the caf," Douglas said when a long, tan building came into sight. "We have a little kitchen in the dorm for snacks, but we eat all our meals here." He pushed open one of the double doors and waved us inside. "We can cut through."

"Oh, man. You *do* have a soft ice-cream machine," I burst out.

Douglas laughed. "And there's a taco bar on Thursdays." He led the way out the main entrance and down the wide stone steps. "The science building is over there. The labs are awesome. A lot of guys looking at med school come here because of that."

"I was only interested in the soft ice-cream machine for scientific purposes," I told him. "I plan to invent some really important ice-cream flavors in the future."

Douglas didn't seem to find that comment especially funny. "The gym's this way." He veered to the left. "The pool meets Olympic standards. Two of the alumni are Olympic medalists."

"That's impressive," Frank said.

"There are impressive alumni from the academy in pretty much every area," Douglas told us. "Medicine, law, finance, whatever. It's a great place to make contacts that you'll use later in your life."

Was it just me? Or did this guy sound like a walking Eagle River Academy catalog?

"That's what my dad says, anyway," Douglas added. "He still does business with a lot of men he met when he went here. It's 'cause you bond when you go through tough things together. That's what my father thinks, anyway."

"All-night study sessions and crazy teachers and all that, huh?" I asked.

"Uh, sort of," Douglas agreed. "It's not just my father who went here," he continued, doing a subject change. "My grandfather, great-grandfather, and even my great-great-grandfather."

Frank and I exchanged a fast look. One of those looks that contain a whole conversation. If you could have heard it, the eyeball convo would have sounded something like this:

Joe's eyeballs: So our friend Douglas doesn't want to talk about the kind of tough situations he and the guys at school bond during. I'm thinking some intensely competitive basket-weaving sessions.

Frank's eyeballs: I'm thinking hazing.

Joe's eyeballs: Yeah, that's what I was thinking too. Don't you have any sense of humor?

SUSPECT PROFILE

Name: Douglas Stillson IV

Hometown: Salem, Massachusetts

Physical description: Age 17, 5'9", 183 lbs., short blond hair, green eyes, freckles.

Occupation: Student

Background: Only boy in family with three girls. Fourth-generation Eagle River Student. Father pushes him very hard to succeed at everything.

Suspicious behavior: Made comment about tough things the guys at school go through, but was evasive about exactly what those things were.

Suspected of: Hazing Roy Duffy, leading to Roy's death.

Possible motive: Willing to do anything to please his father, who is an Eagle River Academy alumnus.

"Whoa," I said. "That's a lot of relatives. What if you'd wanted to go someplace else?"

Douglas looked surprised. "Why would I? It's the best prep school in the country. The waiting list goes on forever. My dad says anyone who wouldn't want to come here is nuts. No offense."

"None taken," Frank told him.

"Good." Douglas nodded. "After the gym, I'll—" His cell went off before he could finish. He pulled it out of his pocket and checked the screen. "I've got to take it. It's my father. I'm sure he wants to know how I did on my calc test."

Frank and I moved onto the grassy lawn next to the walkway to give Douglas a little privacy. But only a little. We're ATAC. That meant we were going to eavesdrop on Douglas's call. You never know where you're going to get an important bit of info.

"I don't know what I got," Douglas said into the phone.

Wow. It didn't sound like his father even bothered with a basic "hi, how are ya" before launching into the grade cross-examination.

"I studied a minimum of an hour and a half a night the week before the test. Five hours the night before," Douglas continued.

"Of course," he replied in answer to something

his dad asked. "Keith studied with me. And we got details on last year's test from a guy who already graduated." Douglas stifled a sigh. "Yeah. I'll call you as soon as I get the test back. Bye."

They hadn't talked about anything not school related. Harsh. I looked around the quad, trying to make Douglas think I was too busy taking in my surroundings to have heard anything he'd said while he was on the phone.

Wait. That tree looked familiar. The way that branch started out going left, then hooked to the right. I glanced over at the building across from me. Colonial style.

I got it. I realized I was standing on the spot where those guys had been playing Frisbee in the ATAC video.

The thought gave me the wiggins again. It made me wonder if I'd be finding myself in other places from the video. Like kneeling on the cement floor at the bottom of Royce Hall. Staring at those dripping red words:

In the cellar, no one can hear you scream.

FRANK

4.

Special Treatment

"I call the bed by the window," Joe announced.

"My stuff is on it. That means it's mine," I told him. I stretched out on the bed by the window. I used my backpack for a pillow and my gym bag for a footrest. That way, Joe couldn't start throwing my gear onto the other bed.

Truth? I didn't really care what bed I had. But I'm the older brother. It's part of my job description to give Joe a hard time once in a while. Besides, the window had a great view of a lake off in the distance.

There was a fast double knock on the door. "It's open," Joe answered.

Open was the only option. I'd noticed there wasn't a lock.

"Hey," Douglas said as he came in. "Just wanted to introduce you to a couple of the other guys. This is Keith Brownlee." He nodded toward a short boy with light brown hair about the color of Joe's. "And that's Wes August." Wes had red hair and eyebrows, and eyelashes so pale they were almost invisible. His skin was really pale too.

Wes flopped down on the end of Joe's bed and kicked off his red Converse sneakers. Keith hoisted himself up and sat on my dresser, and Douglas nabbed one of the two desk chairs.

"Okay, so what's it like to go to a school with girls in it?" Wes asked, grinning.

"Don't ask Frank. He has this weird thing. It's like girls are invisible to him or something," Joe answered.

"They're not invisible," I protested. "I just don't always know what to say to them."

It's true. I see girls. I definitely see them. It's just that when I talk to them, they also see me. And that means they see me blushing. Yes, I actually blush when I talk to girls. So a lot of times I just sort of keep my distance.

JOE

Joe here. I just wanted to say that I wish I could work the blush thing. Girls eat it up. They think it's so cute. They fall all over Frank, the 'shy' boy, even though it is factually true that I am the better looking one.

FRANK

I'm telling this part of the story, Joe. Get out of here.

"Wes has the opposite problem," Keith said. "He thinks he knows exactly what to say—and he says it to every girl he gets near. It doesn't really work for him."

There was another knock on the door. "Enter!" Wes called out.

Two guys walked into the room in silence, their heads down. They carried trays with glasses of soda and bowls of chips.

"Put those on the desk," Keith said. "Then return to the hall and wait for orders."

The boys with the trays obeyed in silence. They

set down the trays and backed out of the room. Yeah, backed out.

Freaky.

"Okay, how do I train Joe to do that?" I asked.

"Fear," Keith answered.

"Those are new guys. It's the first semester here for both of them," Douglas explained. "It's a tradition at the academy that the new guys act as servants for the old guys."

"Yeah. And I am loving every minute of having a personal slave," Wes said. He stood up and wandered over to the chips. "Hey. There's no barbecue chips. I'm deeply disappointed." He grabbed a handful of sour cream and onion, then gave the bowl to me.

"Did you ask for barbecue?" Keith asked.

"Yeah," Wes said as he crunched.

"Call them back in here and make them get you barbecue," Keith instructed.

"It's not such a biggie." He grinned. "But what are servants for, right?" He pounded on the wall with his fist. "Meat! Get in here!" Wes bellowed.

The door swung open one second later, and the two boys entered again, heads lowered.

"I asked for barbecue chips. And I do not see barbecue chips on the tray!" Wes shouted.

"The store was out, so we got—" one of the so-called servants began.

"Did he give you permission to speak?" Keith blasted.

"I didn't hear him give you permission to speak," Douglas cried.

"Both of you. On the floor. Give me fifty," Wes ordered.

The servants dropped down to the ground and started doing push-ups. "Want me to get the bowls of water?" Keith asked.

"Nah. This will work." Wes sat down on the nearest servant, who continued the push-ups with probably a hundred and seventy-five pounds on his back. He cracked up as he rode the guy up and down.

"I'll get the other one!" Keith volunteered. He didn't wait for an answer. He flung himself on top of the second servant. I heard the guy let out a grunt, and his push-up rate slowed down. "No slacking, or I'll give you another fifty," Keith warned him.

I silently counted the push-ups, wanting this to be over. The servant closest to me was really starting to sweat. Dark, wet splotches had appeared on his T-shirt under his arms and around his neck.

The other servant was breathing hard. Long, wheezing breaths that made me want to ask if he needed an inhaler or something.

"That's fifty," Joe said. I realized he'd been counting too.

Wes stood up. "Next time I ask for barbecue, I better get barbecue," he told the servants. "Even if it means firing up the grill and slapping on the sauce yourselves. Now, get out until we call you."

He laughed as the boys backed out of the room. Laughed like he was watching his favorite Adam Sandler movie or something. Was he laughing while Roy Duffy started to have a heart attack?

SUSPECT PROFILE

Name: Wes August

Hometown: New York, New York

Physical description: Age 17, 5'11", 177 lbs., red hair, blue eyes, pale skin

Occupation: Student

Background: Eagle River Academy scholarship student, class clown, only child.

Suspicious behavior: Loves having "servants." Thinks it's funny to hand out punishments to them.

Suspected of: Hazing Roy Duffy, leading to Roy's death.

Possible motives: Wants to fit in with the Eagle Rock Academy guys whose families have gone to the academy from way back. Has a twisted sense of humor.

"You should have let me get the bowls of water," Keith complained.

"Bowls of poop would have been funnier. If we'd had some bowls of poop lying around, I definitely would have used them."

"Bowls?" I repeated. I didn't get how you'd use them with push-ups.

"Yeah. One of the guys who was a senior when I first came here always made us do push-ups with big bowls of water under our faces. We had to completely submerge our heads every time we went down," Keith explained. "One time I didn't go far enough, and the guy held my head under until I saw stars. Actual bright white stars on the inside of my eyelids."

Whoa.

Douglas must have seen the shock on my face. "Like he said, Keith's not doing anything to them that wasn't done to us. You should hear some of my dad's stories about the year he had to be a servant."

"I definitely like being the one to give the orders," Keith said. "It's much sweeter on this side of things."

He sounded as if he really wanted payback for everything that had been done to him. Except he was paying back the wrong people. The new group of servants weren't the ones who had half drowned the guy.

SUSPECT PROFILE

Name: Keith Brownlee

Hometown: Kansas City, Missouri

Physical description: Age 18, 5'5", 159 lbs., light brown hair, brown eyes

Occupation: Student

Background: Picked on in elementary school for being the littlest kid in class; youngest of three brothers; outstanding in math and science.

Suspicious behavior: Encourages harsher punishment of "servants."

Suspected of: Hazing Roy Duffy, leading to Roy's death.

Possible motive: Resents the harsh treatment he got when he was a "servant" and wants to pass it along.

"It is good to be king," Wes agreed. "I think I'm going to make the next servant who messes up wear boxers with hearts on them. Everyone will see them in the locker room."

"Who cares?" Keith asked. "That's not punishment."

"So I guess going through a year as a servant is what you were talking about when you said that at the academy you bond over the tough stuff you go through," Joe said to Douglas.

"What?" Keith shot a sharp look at Douglas. Wes raised his eyebrows.

"Yeah, I guess," Douglas answered. "I mean, going through first year together is part of why the three of us are such good friends."

"True," Wes agreed.

"You can't go through living in fear for a year without getting tight with the guys who are by your side," Keith added. This time he got the what-did-you-just-say look from Douglas.

"Living in fear?" I asked.

"Fear of having your arms fall off from doing too many push-ups," Douglas said quickly.

I didn't believe him.

Joe and I needed a way to get some firsthand information. I popped a chip into my mouth. An idea came to me as I chewed. "So I'm a new guy.

Joe, too. How come we're getting served instead of being servants?" I asked.

"You're only here for two weeks. For the exchange program," Douglas explained. "It doesn't really count."

"The exchange was supposed to give us the total picture of life at the academy," Joe jumped in. He got what I was planning. He pretty much always does.

"Yeah, it doesn't seem fair if we get special treatment," I added. "Do we look like wimps or something?"

Then I waited while Keith, Douglas, and Wes had one of what Joe calls eyeball conversations.

"You want the complete academy experience? You've got it," Keith said. He grabbed the pillow from my bed and yanked off the case.

Then he blindfolded me with it.

Two seconds later my wrists were tied behind my back.

"Neither of you move until we get back," Keith ordered.

5.

In the Cellar, No One Can Hear You Scream

"Great plan, Frank," I whispered.

"Our mission is to find out what really happened to Roy," Frank whispered back. "This is the way to do it. Put ourselves in Roy's position."

"Except for the dead part, let's hope," I said. "It's going to be kind of hard to do information gathering with blindfolds on, don't you think?" I was careful to keep my voice low. "With the not being able to see and everything."

"You knew what I was trying to do—and you helped," Frank pointed out.

"Yeah, because it's a great plan," I admitted.

Frank gave a soft laugh. "We should cut the chatter.

We don't know when they'll be coming back."

I answered with silence. And waited.

And waited.

I hate waiting anyway. But waiting for something bad to happen? Forget about it.

Still, all I could do was wait some more. I felt like someone was stomping around in my stomach. Giving the walls a kick every now and then.

Finally I heard the door open. Then a *swish-swish-swish* sound. And someone pulled me to my feet.

I felt something slide over my head and down my body. Something light and soft. A robe, I realized. Like the ones the guys were wearing in the ATAC video.

Yeah, it was definitely a robe. I could feel it brushing against my legs as . . . somebody walked me out of the room and down a hall. Then down some stairs. Along another hall. Then down some more stairs.

The air was colder now. And I could hear my footsteps—and the footsteps of the other guys—echoing. The cellar. We were walking down the steps into the cellar.

"Kneel!" a voice boomed out.

I didn't recognize the voice. It didn't even sound human.

"Keel!" the inhuman voice commanded again. I realized I hadn't obeyed the first time. Before I could, what felt like a hockey stick whacked me behind the knees. Not that hard. But hard enough to make me drop to the ground.

"You have declared your desire to join the ranks of academy men," The Voice continued. That's how I'd started thinking of it. With a capital T and a capital V. "Academy men are—"

"Fearless!" a chorus of voices shouted.

How many guys were down here with me and Frank? It sounded like at least twenty. Twenty against two. Not exactly the best odds. But two of us were trained ATAC agents. That counted for something.

Right?

"Before you may even consider joining our ranks, you must prove that you are fearless as well," The Voice explained. "You have one chance to refuse the tests that you will be given. That time is now. If you choose to accept the tests of the Order, you will have to face them all. You will either pass, or spend eternity in the cellar with the others who have failed. How do you choose?"

"I accept," Frank said.

"I'm in," I answered.

That's when the chanting started up. Yeah,

chanting. In Latin. At least I'm pretty sure it was Latin. They don't teach Latin at Bayport.

Slowly the chanting died down.

"To begin, you must pay homage to the first member of our Order. Kiss the hand of the Old One," The Voice said over the chanting.

No problem. I didn't think you had to be fearless to pucker up and smooch some old dude's hand. Then I felt the hand. And it was all bone. Not *bony*. Just bone.

The Old One was dead.

And I was holding the hand of his skeleton.

But what could I do? I kissed it. It smelled like dirt. Like it had just been dug up.

The chanting got louder.

"Now one of you must sacrifice blood. It is blood that keeps the Order strong," The Voice proclaimed. "You! The Old One has selected you!"

Hands grabbed my shoulders and my legs. Hands covered my mouth. I was carried away as I heard a long, shrill shriek of pain.

Frank? Was that Frank?

I twisted my body back and forth. I kicked out with my legs. I had to get to my brother. What were they doing to him?

The hands—so many hands—that held me were too strong. I couldn't break free. Even when I heard another howl of agony. Even when the howl cut off abruptly, trailing off into a soft, wet gurgling sound.

Then silence.

Abruptly, all the hands released me, and I tumbled to the ground. I struggled to my feet. And my blindfold was whipped off. Someone untied my wrists.

I scanned my surroundings. I was in a small chamber that had to be just off the main cellar. I hadn't been carried far. Ten figures robed in black stood before me. Their hoods were pulled low, concealing their faces.

And over in the corner . . . I felt my stomach heave. Over in the corner was Frank. Dressed in a white robe, like the one I had on, the hood pulled down to his chin.

"What did you do to him?" I screamed. Frank's robe had a splotch of crimson on the front. A splotch that widened as I watched.

"He was chosen to make the sacrifice," The Voice said. "It is an honor."

I started toward my brother, but two of the black-robed figures blocked my way.

"Now we must all drink, so that his sacrifice will not have been in vain," The Voice continued. The black-robed figure directly across from me pulled a tarnished metal chalice out from behind his back. He raised it to his lips—and drank. When he lowered the cup, I could see his mouth. And it was stained with red.

Blood, I thought. *Frank's blood.*

The figure handed the chalice to me. The metal felt cold in my fingers.

"Drink," The Voice commanded.

I raised the chalice to my lips.

6.

Drink the Blood

I gripped the cold metal chalice with both hands. I couldn't stop myself from looking over at Joe's body lying in the corner. Was he okay? There was so much blood on the white robe. I couldn't see his face. The hood was pulled too low.

"Drink!" the guy with the strange horror-movie voice ordered. I could see his lips under the edge of his hood. They were smeared with red. With blood. Joe's blood.

I raised the cup to my mouth. I figured the best way to help Joe was to follow instructions. Maybe after I drank, they'd let me go over to him.

I forced myself to take a swallow of the blood.

The taste of it made my stomach turn inside out. It wasn't blood. It was . . . I wasn't sure what. There was definitely mayonnaise in the mix. And fish oil. And maybe Tabasco sauce.

What was going on?

One of the guys flung off his hood. Wes. He was laughing. So was everybody else. "You should have seen your face when you tasted the brew!" Wes told me.

I started toward Joe—and this time no one tried to stop me. I dropped to my knees next to him and pulled back his hood. The blank eyes of a CPR practice dummy stared up at me.

The guys around me laughed harder. I laughed too. I couldn't believe they'd psyched me out so good. "Okay, where's Joe?" I asked.

"Right here," Joe answered. He stepped into the side chamber, surrounded by a bunch more guys in black. They all had their hoods off. "They were doing the same thing to me in another room. Happy to see you're not dead, bro."

"Now we're going to par-tay," Keith announced. "And you two are going upstairs with the rest of the servants. They'll take you through the rules of proper behavior," he told me and Joe.

"Come on. I'll take you back up," Douglas said. He led the way back into the main cellar. "We can leave the robes down here." He yanked his off and dropped it on the floor. Joe and I threw ours on top of it. Then we headed up the cellar stairs.

Douglas took us up one more flight of stairs, then down a hall. He opened a door without knocking. The seven guys inside leaped to their feet, lowered their heads, and asked, "What do you desire, sir?"

"Teach these two everything they need to know," Douglas told them. Then he turned and left, closing the door behind him.

The guys immediately all flopped back down on the sofas and chairs scattered around the room. "Welcome to the first-year lounge," one of the boys said. I recognized him as one of the two so-called servants who'd brought the chips and sodas to Joe's and my room earlier. The ones who had to do the push-ups.

"What? No pool table?" Joe asked.

"Just computers and bookshelves," the boy answered. "I'm Bobcat Ellroy, by the way."

The other guy who'd served the chips and stuff with Bobcat laughed. "He's Bobby. The Bobcat thing is a lame attempt to give himself a nickname."

"And he's Keaton. He needs a nickname much worse than I do," Bobby shot back, grinning.

"What are you guys doing in here?" Keaton asked. "An hour ago we were waiting on you. What happened?"

"We told Douglas and the others that we wanted the straight-up Eagle River Academy. We said we wanted to know what it would be like if we'd actually just started here," Joe explained. "A couple minutes later, we were blindfolded and being marched down to the cellar."

That got the attention of pretty much every boy in the lounge. "No way. I'm not hearing this," a guy with curly black hair exclaimed. "You two asked to be servants? When you could have spent two weeks sitting around, ordering us to wipe your heinies?"

"That's something I like to do myself," I answered.

The boy shook his head. "It's true what they say about public school kids. You *are* a lot stupider than we are."

"But more polite," Keaton commented. "As you can tell by Exhibit A over there. Also known as Gabe." He pointed to the black-haired boy who'd basically just called me and Joe idiots.

"So what did we get ourselves in for?" Joe asked. "We heard something about rules for being a perfect servant."

A group groan went up. "They're insane," Gabe told us. "You have to know the name of every one of the masters. That's first, middle, and last. And you have to know a bunch of other garbage about them too. Like the lyrics for every guy's favorite song. Which you have to be able to sing on request."

"You have to wear the right color socks. There's a schedule. You have to memorize it," Bobby added. "And you have to know the years every dean served from the time the academy was founded."

"If you mess up on any of this bull, you get punished," a guy in the back of the room called out.

"Punished?" I repeated. "Punished how?" This could be key. Had Roy died during a punishment?

"Just more drama club productions like what happened in the cellar?" Joe asked.

"They did the blood-drinking thing, right?" Bobby asked. "That's what they started us with."

"Yep," I answered. "It was a little freaky. For a second, I really thought they might have offed Joe."

Joe snorted. "Really? I knew the Frank they showed me was a dummy right away."

My brother is so full of it.

"I almost needed new underwear when they did it to us," Keaton admitted. "But the punishment stuff is usually just whatever they think of at the moment."

"It's almost like a competition among our 'masters,'" Gabe added. "Who can come up with the most original punishment."

"Wes made me eat a whole bag of marshmallows in thirty seconds," Bobby told us. "I took thirty-two, so I had to eat another one."

"Which made him puke," Gabe said. "And then I was ordered to clean it up. With my hands!"

"Nasty," Joe commented.

Completely nasty. But it's not something that would make you have a heart attack.

"Sounds pretty tame to me," I said. "I heard about this kid in Dallas who died during a hazing."

The room went quiet, except for one guy who was still clacking away on a computer keyboard.

I caught Gabe and Bobby exchanging a worried look.

"Yeah, it was a frat thing," Joe jumped in. "The guy's frat brothers put a funnel in his mouth and poured gallons of water down him. Maybe they'd never heard of water poisoning. But the guy still died."

"Like Roy," someone muttered. I couldn't see who.

"Roy had a heart condition," Keaton said.

"Who's Roy?" I asked.

"A first-year guy who died a couple of months ago. Down in the cellar," Gabe answered.

"Not in the cellar. He died in his own bed," Keaton corrected.

"After he was taken down to the cellar for a couple of hours. I still say he was dead when they brought him back upstairs and dumped him in bed," Gabe insisted.

"He was in the cellar alone? None of the rest of you were there?" Joe asked.

"Yeah. Sometimes they choose one of us for a private cellar session," Bobby explained.

"I still say Liam Sullivan brought Roy down there to murder him," the guy working on the computer said, without looking away from the screen.

"Meet David. Our conspiracy theorist. He's probably on one of his favorite conspiracy websites right now," Keaton told us. "Like the one about how it was aliens who really killed Kennedy."

"Or my fave—the one about his inhaler," Bobby added. "Remember that one, David? You thought the government was putting psychedelic drugs in the inhalers of everyone who had asthma as part of some plan to create . . . What was it again?"

"Mutants, like the X-Men," Gabe volunteered.

"Not like the X-Men," David said. He still didn't bother to turn around and really join in the conversation. He was still focused on the computer.

"So what's your theory on Roy? Why would this guy Liam have wanted to kill him, David?" I asked.

"Roy was going out with this girl, Emma. And Liam wanted her for himself," David answered.

"That's pretty extreme," I observed.

"Yeah, well, Liam was pretty extreme about Emma," David answered. "He was, like, almost stalker extreme. P.S., Liam and Emma are together now. So killing Roy worked."

"Roy had a heart attack," Keaton burst out. "The doctor said he had a heart attack!"

"Well, heart attacks can be helped along," David said calmly. "Spend five minutes online and you can come up with a list of drugs that will do it."

SUSPECT PROFILE

Name: Liam Sullivan

Hometown: Madison, Wisconsin

Physical description: Age 17, 5'7", 182 lbs., blond hair, brown eyes

Occupation: Student

Background: Average student; parents made a contribution to the academy to get him in; artistic.

Suspicious behavior: Obsessed with Roy Duffy's girlfriend.

Suspected of: Murdering Roy Duffy and making it look like a hazing incident gone wrong.

Possible motive: Wanted Roy Duffy's girlfriend for himself.

"And in your theory, the other guys just went along with it?" Keaton demanded. "A bunch of them were down there with Liam and Roy. You're saying they just stood around and witnessed a murder?"

"I don't think they even know they witnessed a murder," David explained. "I don't think that kind of conspiracy went down. But I think they all thought they pushed Roy too far. I bet they think they were responsible for giving him a heart attack. Then they were stuck with a dead body. So they decided to just dump Roy in bed and let it look like he died there."

"And none of them told the truth? Not one? I just find that impossible to believe," Keaton said to David.

"Would you want to admit that a guy died while you had him in the cellar, basically torturing him?" David replied. "It's not exactly something that's going to look good on your college applications."

7.

So Dead

"So what do you think?" I asked Frank when we were back in our dorm room. "You think this guy Liam could have set out to give Roy a heart attack?"

"Well, David does seem like the kind of guy who sees a conspiracy behind every tree," Frank answered. "But that doesn't mean he's necessarily wrong about Liam. We definitely need to talk to him. Get some more info."

"Hopefully he'll be in a class with one of us tomorrow," I said. "I'm thinking Keith is a suspect too. He loves the idea of giving back what he got when he was a servant a little too much, don't you think?"

"Yeah. But Wes seemed to really enjoy the idea of having a servant too," Frank commented.

"It seems as if Wes just likes having someone to wait on him, though." I grabbed some chips out of the bowl the guys had left on the dresser. "Who wouldn't want someone to fetch you snacks and clean your room and all that?" We'd found out that another part of our jobs as servants was keeping the masters' rooms in order. Fun, fun.

"True. Keith seemed a lot more about the punishment. Like he wanted to make sure every one of the servants had as hard a time as he did," Frank said. "I can see him getting out of control and pushing Roy too far. I don't think he would have actually meant to kill the guy or anything. But it's not impossible to imagine him letting one of the punishments or rituals get way too dangerous."

I flopped down on my bed. "What's your take on Douglas?"

"That he's trying to be exactly what his dad expects him to be—and that he's not making it," Frank answered.

I nodded. "That's what I got from him too. I can see him taking part in a cover-up. I think he'd do anything not to have to tell his father that he and the guys ended up accidentally killing someone."

"That's all I can see, though," Frank told me. "I don't see Douglas as a guy who would actually push someone so hard it could hurt them."

"Wes either," I said. "Although that dude kind of has a twisted sense of humor. If he thought something was funny, he might take it too far."

"Those servant jokes of his were definitely sick," Frank agreed.

I let my head hang over the edge of the bed. I think the increased blood flow makes me think better. Plus, it feels kind of good. "So I say we put Liam on the top of our suspect list—at least until we get more info. Then Keith. With Wes and Douglas coming in tied for third."

"I think I might put Wes ahead of Douglas, instead of tied with him." Frank didn't hang his head over the edge of the bed. He says it gives him a headache, and the headache stops him from being able to think at all.

"Douglas is really tightly wound, though. Sometimes those are the guys who just lose it," I commented. I could almost feel my face turning redder.

"But Wes isn't tightly wound enough," Frank countered. "That's just as bad. If you think everything's a big joke, is there anything you won't do?"

"Like kill someone?" I asked. "Nobody kills another person just for laughs."

"If they're a psychopath, they do." Frank's face was solemn. Even though I was looking at him upside down, I could tell he was worried. "We need to keep watching—"

The door swung open before he could finish. I sat up so fast I got a head rush.

A tall man with his brown hair in a short ponytail stepped into the room and gave us a half salute. I noticed he had a couple of scars on his palm. Just raised white slashes.

"I'm Mr. Diehl," the man said. "I teach history—World and European—here at the academy. I'm also in charge of this dorm. I just wanted to introduce myself and say welcome." He shifted his weight from foot to foot. "So, welcome."

"Thanks. I'm Frank Hardy, and that's my brother, Joe."

Frank's always on top of introductions and other politeness kinds of stuff. I space sometimes. It makes Aunt Trudy crazy. She says I'm going to convince people I was raised by bears.

Which actually, it might have been cool if I was. Think about it.

"I have an office up on the third floor. You'll see

my name on the door. My quarters are next to it," Mr. Diehl told us. "Come find me if you need anything."

"Thanks," I said.

Mr. Diehl headed back out the door. But he hesitated before he closed it. "I know you boys are here to see what life at this type of school is like. And I think that's a great idea." As he spoke, I realized he had a few scars on his face, too. They were so faint you didn't notice them right away, but one of them cut through his eyebrow. A quarter inch lower, and Mr. Diehl might have lost his eye.

"I do. I think it's a very good idea. You boys—all you boys—should know what kind of options are available. I hope Andrew and Jamie will tell all the other students about their time at public school. But . . ."

He glanced back and forth between me and Frank, then continued. "But there are some traditions at the academy . . . no, traditions isn't exactly the word I'm looking for. Although they were going on back when I was a student here—so maybe that is the right word. Anyway, there are things that happen at the academy that I don't think have any place at a school. Things that I don't think make for an environment conducive to learning. I don't want you to think that I approve of these things. Even though the administration encourages the faculty to turn a blind eye."

I nodded. Even though he wasn't being very clear.

"What I'm trying to say is, if there is something you are asked to do that makes you uncomfortable, you can refuse," Mr. Diehl told us. "So—good night, then." And he was gone, closing the door behind him with a soft click.

"I hope he's clearer when he teaches his history classes," I said. "But he had to have been talking about hazing, don't you think?"

"Yeah. Unless there's something else ugly going down around here," Frank agreed. "It's kind of creepy what he said about the administration encouraging the teachers to—what did he call it?"

"Turn a blind eye," I answered. "Yeah. But remember how Dean McCormack told Mom and Dad and us that he was a student here. Maybe he's kind of like Keith. Maybe he thinks if he went through the servant thing, everyone should have to. Or he's like Douglas's dad and thinks it's part of the bonding that leads to all those great business contacts later."

"Makes sense." Frank picked up the giant black binder Keaton had given us. "We better get started memorizing the song lyrics and all that other junk we're supposed to have cold by tomorrow morning."

"Yeah," I agreed. "I don't want any of the potential psychopaths coming up with punishments for me."

I watched Liam Sullivan. He was sitting one row over and two seats down from me in my world history class. I was pretty sure he was doodling and not taking notes as Mr. Diehl lectured. I couldn't see his notebook from where I was sitting. But the way his hand was moving gave him away.

Liam wasn't the only guy in class who wasn't exactly paying attention to Mr. Diehl. Keith and another boy were playing hangman behind me, and I was pretty sure I could hear somebody snoring a little in the back row.

Mr. Diehl had given a few pleas for attention, but they hadn't worked. He was one of that kind of teacher. The kind who just give off this vibe that says you-don't-have-to-do-what-I-say-because-I'm-never-gonna-do-anything-about-it.

"That's not the way you spell that," Keith whispered.

"How do you know? It's not like it's in the dictionary," the guy he was playing hangman against whispered back.

Mr. Diehl called on Liam. When he stood up to answer, I got a look at his notebook. Yep, I was right. He'd been . . . well, not doodling. The drawing of the girl's face that covered one whole page was way too good to be called a doodle.

I wondered if the girl was supposed to be Emma. The Emma who was formerly Roy Duffy's girlfriend.

Yeah, it was. I spotted the name Emma written sideways next to the drawing. Emma was definitely cute.

But that wasn't enough evidence to convict Liam of murder.

I didn't have any more time to think about Emma and Liam, because it was my turn to answer one of Mr. Diehl's questions. And I got it right, thank you very much.

Then the bell rang, and we were outta there. World history was the last class of the day, so I headed to the dorm. I was wondering whether Frank had found out anything interesting, when I heard someone behind me shout, "Freeze, new meat!"

I froze.

Liam Sullivan circled around in front of me. "Do you know who I am?" he asked.

"Liam Alexander Sullivan," I answered. A couple of other masters stopped to take in the action.

"And what's my favorite color?" Liam asked, eyes narrowed.

"Green."

Liam started to shake his head.

"That's lime green," I quickly added. "As opposed to forest or sea foam." I sent out a silent thank-you to Frank for keeping me up until four a.m. studying the big black binder of everything a slave had to know.

"And my favorite song?" Liam demanded.

"'Bohemian Rhapsody,'" I said, praying he wasn't going to make me sing it. Have you ever heard that song? If you haven't, you need to know that it is long. As in looong. There was no way I was going to get through it without messing up on the lyrics. No possible way.

"Sing it," Liam told me.

I was so dead.

8.

Dirty Socks

"I thought I was dead," Joe told me as we headed into the dorm together. He'd caught up to me as I was heading up the hill to the building. "I could only come up with two words. Mama. And Beelzebub."

"Mama and Beelzebub. That could be the name of a new song," I joked.

"You wouldn't have thought it was funny if you were the one surrounded by masters while having an intense brain freeze," Joe complained.

"But he only made you do a push-up. And that's it?" I asked.

"Yeah." Joe shook his head. "How psycho is that? And in a good way. Not in a raving-psychopath-who-killed-a-guy-to-get-his-girlfriend way."

"Maybe he could just tell that one push-up for your puny arms is like a couple hundred for a regular person," I suggested. Because I'm the big brother. It's my job to say things like that.

Joe socked me in the arm. "So clearly he's not a guy who gets off on doling out the punishments. Not the way Keith does. But there is one thing about Liam, though. He's definitely into that Emma chick. He spent all history class drawing her picture."

We started up the stairs to our floor. "Maybe we need to talk to Emma herself."

"Frank Hardy, wanting to talk to an actual girl?" Joe gasped in mock horror. "How are we supposed to make *that* happen?" he continued in his regular voice. "In the first place, it's an all-guys school—in case you haven't noticed."

"There's a dance tonight. I guess no one bothered to tell you about it," I explained. I opened the door to our room and stuck my backpack under the desk on my side. Joe threw his onto his bed. He's a total slob. I had to remake the bed he'd made for one of the masters this morning. When my brother was finished, it looked like he'd made the bed with the master still in it.

"A dance, huh?" Joe asked, flinging himself down next to the backpack. "Sweet."

"Not so sweet for us servants," I told him. "Keaton gave me the rundown. Servant types aren't allowed to dance. We are allowed to serve punch and whatever else the masters can think of."

"How do the guys survive a year of this?" Joe asked. "No dancing. No TV. No use of the pool table. Just memorizing pages and pages of worthless info and making sure the chip bowls are filled."

I ignored his complaining. There are times where ignoring Joe is the best course of action. "I figure Emma's definitely going to be there with Liam," I said. "We just need to find a few minutes to talk to her alone."

"Maybe I could spill punch on her and talk to her while I clean it off," Joe suggested.

"And earn yourself a night in the cellar," I answered. "Keaton told me that's what they do if you really screw up. All the masters spend the whole night working over one slave. It was a night like that when Roy died."

"Sounds like you two had a lot of time to talk," Joe said.

"Yeah, we were in bio together. Andrew is usually his lab partner, so I am while we're here," I explained.

"He say anything else of use?" Joe shoved his sneakers off without bothering to untie them and let them fall to the floor.

"Just that Roy earned his private night in the cellar by screwing up on ironing Liam's shirts. There was a crease that Liam claimed Roy had put in one of them on purpose."

"Liam *so* didn't seem like a guy who'd go off about something like that today," Joe said. "Like I told you, I got one push-up from him."

"Yeah, but you don't have a girlfriend he wants," I reminded my brother. "You don't have *any* girlfriend."

"I like to spread the love around," Joe shot back.

"Right."

"You doubt me?" Joe exclaimed. "You actually—"

He stopped in midsentence. I didn't have to ask why. Keith was shouting, almost loudly enough to make the walls shake.

"I don't want to hear your excuses, David!" I heard him scream. "I don't want to hear one more word. In fact, get your socks off and get them in your mouth. Then give me jacks until I tell you to stop."

Joe sat up. He shot me a look. "Do you think Keith knows David has asthma?" he asked.

"Both socks!" Keith yelled from the hallway. "Now start 'em up."

"We'd better get out there," I said. "Exercising while being gagged with socks would make it hard for *anyone* to breathe. Forget about an asthmatic." I threw open the door, and Joe and I rushed out.

David was doing jumping jacks in the middle of the hall. Keith was setting the pace by calling out, "One, two, one, two." He was really making David work. David's face was already turning red, and I could see beads of sweat forming around his hairline and on his upper lip.

"Get a good look," Keith told me and Joe, pausing in the counting. "This is what happens when you aren't able to follow simple instructions." He whipped his head back toward David. "Don't slow down, meat. You do, and you'll earn yourself a night in the cellar you'll never forget. One, two, one, two, onetwo, onetwo, onetwo."

One of the socks in David's mouth started to come out. Keith used two fingers to jam it back in, shouting out the count for the jumping jacks the whole time.

I wanted to knock Keith to the ground. I wanted to jam his own socks all the way down his throat. But I just watched. Joe and I just watched. Because we had to act like good little servants, at least for now. It was how we were going to find out what really happened to Roy.

Joe elbowed me and nodded to the staircase. Mr. Diehl was coming up. Perfect. He'd shut down Keith.

Except he didn't. As I watched, he turned around and headed back down the stairs. And he'd seen what Keith was doing to David. I was sure of it. What was his deal? He'd made such a point of telling me and Joe that we didn't have to go along with anything we didn't want to.

But then there was that blind eye thing . . .

A door opened down the hall, and Douglas and one of the other masters walked out. Douglas's eyes widened slightly at the sight of David. He was looking bad. His face wasn't just flushed now. It was splotchy—some parts an angry brick red, and some a sickly pale.

"Hey, Keith," Douglas called. "We're going to watch the Knicks game we TiVoed last night. You coming? It looks like the meat has been tenderized enough."

"Aw, is Dougie feeling sorry for the little servant?" Keith asked in a baby voice. "I don't think Dougie's daddy would like that. Dougie's daddy wants his little boy to grow up strong."

For a moment Douglas's face started to look almost like David's—a horrible mix of pasty and deep red. Then he swallowed hard. He moved closer to David and watched him with cold eyes. "What'd he do, anyway?" Douglas asked Keith.

"He got me a blue toothbrush," Keith answered.

"What a moron!" Douglas exploded. Spittle flew out of his mouth as he continued to shout. "Everyone knows you hate blue. Totally everyone!"

It was like something in his brain had snapped.

"Give me a squat between each jack," Douglas commanded David.

"Good one!" Keith exclaimed. He slapped hands with Douglas. Douglas grinned.

And David began to wheeze. With every breath he took. Was he about to have an asthma attack?

"Listen to the guy," Joe said loudly. "How out of shape is he? A few minutes of exercise, and he's gasping for air."

I thought I knew what Joe was doing. I just hoped it worked.

"Yeah. You private school guys are kind of wimpy," I added. "You wouldn't last a day at our school."

"Let's see how tough you two are. Get your socks off your feet and into your mouths and get moving," Douglas ordered.

Keith laughed. "Yeah. Join the party, boys."

I noticed the *thud-thud* of David's jumping jacks

slow down as I pulled off my shoes. Keith and Douglas didn't seem to notice. Neither of them shouted at David to keep moving.

Perfect. That meant Joe and me joining the "party" was giving David a little bit of a break. Joe's plan had worked.

I shoved my socks in my mouth. I was very glad that—unlike my brother—I change my socks every day. I was betting Joe was chomping on at least three days of foot crud right now.

I started doing the jumping jack/squat combo. And I made sure to do it badly. Wobbly on the squats. Doing the jacks way too slow. Joe gave a performance that was just as bad. We had Keith, Douglas, and the other master right in our faces. Screaming at us to shape up.

Out of the corner of my eye, I shot a quick glance at David. He looked better. Less like he was going to collapse at any second.

"All right! That's it!" Keith finally yelled. "Get yourselves to your rooms and wait for more orders." He turned to Douglas and the other master. "Let's go watch that game. We can at least see part of it before we have to go to dinner."

The three of them headed for the stairs. David got his socks out of his mouth first. He jerked an inhaler from his pocket and took a long suck.

"You okay?" Joe mumbled as he spat out his socks.

"Yeah. Or I will be." David took another pull on the inhaler. "Thanks to you two. That was pretty stupid of you, by the way. You were pretty much begging for an all-night session in the cellar," he told us. "And that's something you really don't want," he added as he headed toward his room.

I walked back into Joe's and my room and headed directly for the dresser. I needed a new pair of socks.

"You're putting those back on?" I asked as I spotted Joe putting his drooled-on socks back on his feet.

"I'm taking a shower before the dance," he answered. "I'll put clean ones on after that."

Unbelievable.

"What did you think of that Dr. Jekyll and Mr. Hyde routine Douglas pulled out there?" Joe continued.

"Keith knew exactly how to work him," I commented. "All he had to do was say that Douglas's dad wouldn't approve of Douglas taking it easy on a servant—and *wham*. Like you said, Jekyll to Hyde."

"Seeing him with David, it wasn't that hard to imagine Douglas pushing Roy until he had a heart attack," Joe said.

"I thought Douglas and Keith were going to let David have an asthma attack right in front of them," I agreed.

"Let him? Forget about let him. They were going to *make* him have one." Joe tied his sneakers.

"At least you thought to have them get focused on us. That was smart, bro." I tied my sneakers too.

"We had to do something. It's not like Mr. Diehl was going to. Can you believe him?" Joe asked. "He practically ran back down the stairs when he saw what Keith was doing to David."

"And after he made it sound like we could go to him for help." I shook my head.

"He might not have been that much help even if he had come up," Joe said. "Did you end up having a class with the guy?"

"Huh-uh. Why?" I asked.

"He's one of those teachers that nobody pays attention to. Guys were playing hangman. Liam was doing that drawing of Emma. Somebody was snoozing. And Diehl didn't even say anything to anyone," Joe answered.

"Let's go upstairs and talk to him," I suggested. "Maybe he knows something about what really happened to Roy. Maybe that's why he made such a point of telling us we didn't have to go along with anything we didn't want to."

"So he might know that hazing led to Roy's death. Or even that somebody killed Roy—and didn't even say anything." Joe rolled his eyes. "That is extreme wimp behavior."

"Yeah, but so is the behavior you saw in Diehl's class today, right?" I asked. "He couldn't even tell a kid to wake up and pay attention."

"You're right. Let's get up there." Joe led the way into the hall and up the stairs. We quickly found the door with Mr. Diehl's name on it and knocked.

No answer.

"I guess we'll have to come back," Joe said.

"Or . . ."

"Or we could possibly find out *more* if we go in and have a look around when Diehl's not there," Joe finished my thought.

I tried the door. Unlocked. So we went on in.

Joe headed for the desk. I headed for the filing cabinet in the corner. I wanted to see if Diehl had files on the guys in the dorm. But the cabinet was locked.

"Anything interesting over there?" I asked Joe.

He held up a bottle of prescription medication. "Diehl takes BuSpar."

"That's an anti-anxiety med," I said.

"He also smokes." Joe pointed to a pack of cigarettes on the desk.

"What's in the notebook?" I asked. I nodded toward the thick, worn notebook next to the cigarettes.

Joe opened it and did a quick flip-through. "Jackpot! This is all about hazing. It's a record of everything that goes down between the servants and the masters. Listen to this."

He began to read. "November third. Another cellar night. One of the worst so far. The masters found rats someplace. Maybe a pet store. Maybe they trapped them. They tied the servants' hands and feet together. Then smeared peanut butter on them. And left them down there. With the rats."

I could almost feel the rats running over my own skin. Those little claws. And those teeth. The sharp, yellow teeth. "We got off easy last night," I commented.

"Yeah. Big-time," Joe answered. He turned the page. "November fifth," he began to read again.

"Wait. Skip to the night Roy died. February thirteenth," I told him.

"Right." Joe began thumbing through the pages, then froze. "Do you hear that?"

I listened for a second. "Yeah," I answered. "Someone's coming."

Joe closed the notebook and put it back next to

the cigarettes. He circled around in front of the desk, just as the door swung open.

"Oh, hello," Mr. Diehl said.

"Hey. We wanted to ask you something, so we decided to come in and wait. I hope that's okay," I told him.

"Sure. Have a seat." He waved at the chairs in front of his desk. Joe and I sat. "So, um, what can I do for you?"

I wanted to flat-out ask him why he'd ignored what Keith had done to David. Mr. Diehl had to know that David had asthma. That's definitely something a teacher in charge of a dorm would know about a kid who lived in that dorm.

But that didn't feel like the way to go. Sometimes it's easier to find out what you need to know if you don't ask directly.

SUSPECT PROFILE

Name: Geoffrey Diehl

Hometown: Oakland, CA

Physical description: Age 29, 5'9", 190 lbs., thinning brown hair, brown eyes

Occupation: History teacher

Background: Former Eagle River Academy student, takes anti-anxiety medication, single

Suspicious behavior: Keeps careful watch on the hazing activities at the academy but does nothing to stop dangerous hazing.

Suspected of: Criminal negligence. Doing nothing to stop the death of Roy Duffy.

Possible motive: Afraid to take action against hazing because the academy administration encourages the faculty to turn a blind eye.

"We saw something we think you should know about," I said. "Joe and I don't like to snitch—"

"But we think we have to this time," Joe jumped in. "Because somebody could die."

"What happened?" Mr. Diehl asked.

As if he had no idea.

"Keith made David do jumping jacks with his mouth stuffed with socks," I told him. "And David's asthmatic. He looked this close to passing out." I held up two fingers pressed together.

"That's definitely something I need to know about," Mr. Diehl answered. "You did the right thing to come to me. I'll handle it."

Right. Like he handled it when it was happening right in front of his face.

"I'll inform the dean tomorrow," he promised us.

But could we believe him?

9.

Psycho Boyfriends

Boarding school dances aren't so different from public school dances. Still in a gym. Still a lot of crepe paper. Low lights. Bored chaperones. A bunch of couples dancing. But also herds of nondancing males and herds of nondancing females, looking at each other.

"There she is," I told Frank. "That's Emma Whitley."

"And I'm guessing that guy she's glued against is Liam," Frank commented.

"Wow, are you some kind of detective or something?" I asked.

Frank didn't laugh. Most of the time, Frank

doesn't laugh at my jokes. That's because Frank has no sense of humor.

FRANK

Frank here. I've said it before, and clearly I must say it again: I have a perfectly fine sense of humor. My brother just isn't funny. Now I'm out of here. This isn't my section.

JOE

"So what's the plan?" Frank asked. "We need to get Emma away from Liam at some point. She's not going to want to talk about how much Liam hated Roy with Liam standing right there."

"We need to stake out the girls' bathroom," I answered.

Frank raised his eyebrows.

The guy really doesn't know much about girls. "Because your average girl goes to the bathroom about five times during a dance," I explained. "It's all about the lip gloss and the talking to the other girls. And it's one place no girl brings her boyfriend."

"Okay, let's get into position," Frank said.

We circled around the gym and stationed ourselves fairly close to the bathroom door. Plenty close enough to easily intercept Emma. But not so close anyone would think there was something wrong with us.

About two minutes later I had to go to the bathroom myself. Bad. There was something about watching one, I guess. "Be right back," I told Frank.

I hurried into the guys' bathroom and almost turned right back around. Mr. Diehl was totally tearing into Gabe. It's bad enough to have a teacher go off on you. You really don't need an audience.

But they'd both already seen me. So I did the best thing I could think of. I ducked into the nearest stall. That way, Gabe could at least pretend I wasn't there. And, hey, I *did* need to go.

"Do you understand what I'm saying to you?" Diehl continued, as if he hadn't been interrupted. "Cigarettes are filth and they fill you with filth. I don't ever want to see you with one again. I'll go straight to the dean if I do."

Guess the administration didn't encourage the faculty to turn a blind eye to smoking. But it struck me as odd that Diehl, a smoker himself—I remembered the cigarettes we'd found in his office—

would come down so hard on Gabe for doing the same thing. Just another case of the old "Do as I say, not as I do" routine some adults pull on kids, I guessed.

I heard Gabe mutter something. Then I heard footsteps and the sound of the door opening and closing. A few seconds later more footsteps, and the door opening and closing again.

Wonder if Frank had to start talking to Emma by himself, I thought as I washed my hands. If he *was* attempting to talk to Emma, he was going to be blushing and getting all tongue-tied.

I headed back out into the gym and over to Frank as quickly as I could, in case he needed an assist.

Nope. He was still solo.

I glanced over at the spot on the dance floor where I'd last seen Liam and Emma. Yep. Still there.

"Hey, you're the exchange student guys, right?"

I turned around and saw a girl standing there. Short black hair. Beauty mark on one side of her mouth.

"That's us," I told her.

"Well, since you don't know any girls around here, I've decided that you'll be my charity cases," she said. "Which of you wants to dance with me first? Oh, I'm Lil, in case you want to know."

"I definitely would want to be first. And second. And third," I answered. "But Frank and I aren't supposed to dance. We—"

Lil rolled her eyes. "That ridiculous masters and servants game, right?"

"It's not exactly . . . I wouldn't . . . It's not a game," Frank managed to get out.

"Ignore my brother," I said. "He's been like this all night. He can't stop staring at that girl." I pointed out Emma. "He thinks he's in love or something."

Lil studied Frank for a minute. "Give it up," she told him. "I'm sorry, but you just don't look psycho enough for Emma. I should know. She's my next-door neighbor at the dorm."

Jackpot. I was hoping Lil would spill some info about Emma—since I couldn't take her up on her offer of a dance. And how wrong was that, by the way? A cute girl actually asking me to dance, and I had to say no.

"He's kind of psycho—in his own quiet way," I assured Lil. "What kind of psycho does Emma like?"

"The kind of extremely needy psycho who decides he can't live without her," Lil said. "First there was Noah, who wrote her two poems a day. Which was upped to five when she said she wanted to break up with him. Five tearstained poems of patheticness."

She shook her head. "Then there was Roy. I don't want to speak ill of the dead, but Roy was twisted."

The little hairs on the back of my neck stood up. We were about to find out something important.

"Twisted how?" I asked.

"Emma wanted to break up with him, too." Lil turned to Frank. "That's the other thing. Em's always wanting to break up. You really don't want to get gooey about her."

"Okay," Frank said.

"So anyway, Emma wanted to break up with Roy," Lil continued. "She was ready to move on to Liam, psycho number three, who she's dancing with right now. But Roy didn't want to break up with her. And that's where the psycho part came in. Roy actually blackmailed Emma into staying with him."

"Sick!" I burst out.

"So sick," Lil agreed. "Roy had helped Emma cheat on this bio test. He helped her figure out how to do it. Then, when she wanted to kick him to the curb, he said he'd go to our school's dean and tell her what they had done."

"Sick and cold," I said.

"Yeah." Lil shook her head again. "Especially

because Roy knew our school has this zero-tolerance policy about cheating. He knew that if he ratted out Emma, she would have been expelled. He also knew enough about Emma's parents to know that if that happened, her life would become a complete waking nightmare."

"So she stayed with him?" Frank asked. His curiosity about our case had clearly won out over his girl shyness. He wasn't blushing or stammering or anything. Atta boy, Frankster.

"Until he died," Lil answered. "But she hooked up with Liam about two seconds later. Very classy. Not that Roy deserved loyalty or anything after what he did to her. Which brings us to psycho number three."

"Liam," I said.

"Liam." Lil rolled her eyes. "He's not an especially interesting kind of psycho. Just your basic extremely jealous one. He's always flying into a tantrum because he thinks Em is looking at some other guy. Or some other guy is looking at her. Or whatever. I don't—"

Lil stopped in midsentence. "This is my favorite song ever. Are you sure one of you won't break the rules and dance with me?"

"Can't," Frank said.

"Sorry. So sorry you can't even know how sorry," I told her.

She smiled at us. "Okay, well, I can't not dance to this song, so, gotta go." She whirled off into the crowd of people on the dance floor.

"Wow," I said.

"Yeah, she just gave us a new suspect. I think Emma has to go on our list," Frank answered.

"True. But that's not what I meant," I told him. "I just meant wow, how cool was Lil?"

"The thing about Emma is that even though she had motive, it would have been really hard for her to get into the dorm the night Roy died—or was killed," Frank went on.

"Of course, Liam lives in the dorm. And he might have been very happy to help Emma if she decided she had to off blackmailer Roy," I added.

"He does seem pretty attached," Frank agreed, looking over at the two-headed body that was Liam and Emma dancing together.

"Extremely." I spotted Lil in the crowd. She seemed totally happy dancing by herself. Joining up with a couple briefly. Weaving through a circle of other girls for a minute.

"Here she comes," Frank said.

"She's way over there," I told him.

"I'm talking about *Emma*."

Oh, right. Emma. The whole reason we were lurking by the girls' bathroom.

"Emma! You and Liam looked great out there!" I called.

She stopped. "Do I know you?" she asked. But not in a snotty way. In a kind of teasing, flirty way.

"I'm Joe Hardy. My brother Frank and I are part of an exchange student program. We're going to Eagle River and living in Liam's dorm for a couple of weeks," I told her.

"Cool," she answered as she came toward us. "How do you like it so far?"

"Great. Except for the being a servant part," I answered.

For a moment Emma didn't answer, and I thought her face got a little paler. "Yeah, that part sucks. But then you get to be a master the next year."

"Except for Roy," Frank said. "We heard about what happened to him. That must have been really hard on you."

Emma's smile slid off her face. "Yeah, Roy. This probably sounds horrible, but I try not to think about him. It just hurts too much."

"It doesn't sound *that* horrible." I touched her arm.

"Hey!" Emma pasted the smile back on her face. "My school is doing a Boys of Eagle River calendar. It's for charity. Would you guys want to be in it? It's for charity," she said again. "And you're definitely both cute enough to be models."

I almost got whiplash from that subject change. She really, really, really didn't want to talk about Roy.

SUSPECT PROFILE

Name: Emma Whitley

Hometown: Boston, Massachusetts

Physical description: Age 17, 5'5", 130 lbs., long brown hair, blue eyes

Occupation: Student

Background: Girlfriend of Liam Sullivan; former girlfriend of Roy Duffy; both parents college professors

Suspicious behavior: Gets extremely agitated when talking about Roy, does anything to change the subject.

Suspected of: Murder of Roy Duffy with the help of Liam Sullivan

Possible motive: Wanted to stop Roy from blackmailing her.

"Sure, Frank and I have always talked about how we want to be models," I told Emma.

Frank shot me a look of extreme pain. I ignored him. This could give us more time to spend with Emma. Time we could use to get more info about her and Roy.

"Cool. Ultracool," Emma answered.

"But we're not going to be around for very long," Frank said.

I thought he was about to blow it, but I underestimated him. "When can we get in a photo shoot?" he asked. For my brother, that was like asking when he could get in a root canal.

"Um." Emma hesitated. "Well . . ." Clearly she had no real interest in us as calendar boys.

I spotted Lil twirling past. "Hey, Lil!" I called out. She boogied on over.

"Emma just recruited me and Frank for your school calendar," I told her.

"Excellent!" she answered. "I would love to take your picture. I'm the photographer for the gig. Can you come by tomorrow afternoon?"

"Absolutely," Frank told her. He looked over at Emma. "Will you be there?"

"Of course she'll be there," Lil told us. "She's the stylist. Just go to Edwards Hall. Someone will call for us."

"We'll be there," I told her.

FRANK

10.

Model Behavior

Emma Whitley ran her fingers through my hair. "You've got great texture," she said.

"I've always thought that about Frank," Joe said from the chair next to mine in the downstairs lounge at Emma and Lil's dorm.

I felt myself blushing. Of course. It didn't help that what felt like about a hundred girls were watching Emma "style" me. It was probably only about twenty. But still.

I hoped that at some point during the photo shoot Joe or I would manage to get a couple of minutes alone with Emma to talk to her about Roy. Otherwise, this afternoon was going to be a waste.

And something Joe would probably be teasing me about for the next few years of my life.

"Wait. What are you doing now?" I burst out. Emma had finished futzing around with my hair and now had a sponge way too close to my face.

"Just a little foundation," she told me.

"Yeah, you really need it," Lil added. "Not just you. All the models. Otherwise you'll look totally washed out."

"I can live with that," I answered.

"Oh, come on, Frank," Joe said. "I let them put it on me."

I snorted. As if following Joe in this situation was a good thing.

"Pretty please," Emma said, moving the sponge an eighth of an inch closer to my face.

"Fine," I said. A second later I felt the cold stuff spreading over my skin.

"So who are the other guys you want to be in the calendar?" Joe asked.

"Li-am," four or five of the girls watching chorused.

"Emma would have Liam for every month if she could," Lil added.

"Does that mean last year's was all Roy?" I queried.

A bunch of the girls looked at me like I was a huge jerk. Emma looked shocked.

I knew it was a completely uncool question, but Joe and I needed to get the convo over to Roy somehow.

"This was Roy's first year at Eagle River," Emma finally said.

"How did you two meet, anyway?" I asked, pretending I just had no idea how uncomfortable I was making her. Uncomfortable people sometimes say things they don't mean to. Things like the truth.

"I don't even remember," Emma said as she finished up applying the makeup to my face. I noticed her fingers were trembling a little. "Because I was so little. My parents and Roy's have known each other forever."

So Roy definitely would have known how strict Emma's parents were. He would have known just how much trouble she'd have gotten in if the fact that she'd cheated on that bio test had come out.

"I'm done here," Emma told Lil. "I have a ton of studying to do. You care if I skip the actual picture-taking part of the shoot? These guys are ready."

"Won't they need touch-ups?" Lil asked.

Emma had already started walking away. "I want their hair messy," she said over her shoulder. "Just slap some powder on their faces if they start to get shiny."

Then she was out of sight.

Had she bolted because I'd made her feel sad about Roy? Or because she was still mad at Roy and didn't want it to show?

Or was it because she felt guilty for murdering the guy?

"Where have you two been?" Keith demanded from the TV lounge as Joe and I walked into the dorm. It was almost dinnertime. The bus back from the girl's school had taken a while to come.

"Didn't Liam tell you?" Joe asked.

Liam turned his head. "How was I supposed to know where you were? All I knew was you weren't here to get the chips. And there were only about thirty other servants who could do it for us. I was most vexed." He grinned at us.

"This is serious, Liam," Keith snapped. "They broke the rules. Servants are supposed to come straight back to the dorm as soon as class lets out."

"One push-up for each of them," Liam said. He turned back to the TV. He and Keith were the only two guys using the lounge.

Keith stood up. "So where were you?" he asked again.

"Emma and Lil had us go over to their school," Joe said. "I guess they wanted some new faces for their calendar."

"Wait. Emma?" Liam exclaimed. He was on his feet too. "Emma, as in my Emma?"

"If *your* Emma is Emma Whitley, then yeah," Joe answered. "I guess she thought Frank and I were cute or something. She's the one who asked us if we wanted to be in the calendar."

I watched Liam carefully. If he was the jealous type, what Joe had said to him would get him very jealous. The muscles in his neck tightened a little, but that was it.

"Hardys," David called from halfway up the stairs. "You have a phone call on the pay phone. Sounds parental."

"If it's parents, you better take it," Keith said. "But from now on, you have four minutes to get back here after the final bell rings. You're late, you suffer."

I nodded, then Joe and I headed up the stairs and over to the pay phone. It had been hung up.

"What's the deal?" Joe asked. "Do they want us to call them back?"

"The deal is that you saved my life and I owed you one," David answered. "I heard what you were saying to Liam about his girlfriend. I'm sure the guy was wanting to massacre you until I got you out of his sight."

"Just 'cause we told him she wanted us for the calendar?" I asked. "A lot of guys are in it, right?"

"Liam can't take it if another guy even says Emma's name," David answered. "He had a crush on her from day one of the semester."

"Wasn't she with Roy back then?" Joe asked.

"Yeah. Like that mattered to him," David answered. "You should see his room. I'm the one who has to clean it. It's like the Emma Whitley shrine. He has a million pictures of her and a box full of all this other garbage. Practically everything she's ever touched, he has. Even some old tests and study notes."

Tests and study notes. Could that possibly be the stuff Roy was using to blackmail Emma?

Did Liam have it because he'd killed Roy to get it back for her?

"So, do you think you've completely paid us back for saving your life?" I asked David. "Or do you think you can do us one more favor?"

David raised his eyebrows. "Depends on the favor."

"Next time you're in Liam's room, you think you could borrow that box of stuff and let us have a look at it?" I asked.

"Why?" David asked.

Good question. I didn't have a good answer.

"Frank's completely in looove," Joe said. "He probably wants to smell the ink on her notes or something."

I shrugged. "Kinda," I said.

"Whatever," David said. "I have to go turn down Liam's bed anyway. He likes me to leave a box of Milk Duds on his pillow. I can get it for you then. But I need it back before lights out."

"You got it," I told him.

"I'll drop it by your room," David said. Then he took off.

"A box of clues by special delivery," Joe said. "Excellent."

11.

Box of Clues

Frank and I headed to our room to change socks. There are special socks servants are required to wear for dinner.

If you must know, white with red polka dots. Happy now?

I spotted Mr. Diehl coming down the hall from the opposite direction. I checked to make sure no one else was around. Nope. So when he got close enough, I said, "Hey, Mr. Diehl. How did it go with the dean? Were you able to talk to him?"

"No." Mr. Diehl rubbed the scar that ran through his eyebrow. "His schedule was jammed today. I barely got to speak to his secretary when I dropped by his office. And I just tried him on the phone. Sometimes he works late. He wasn't there, but I left him a voice-mail message."

Frank nodded. "That's great. We just don't want anything bad to happen, with David having that health condition and everything."

"I don't want that either," he agreed. "I'll get back to you both once I hear from Dean McCormack."

"Thanks," I told him. Frank and I went into our room. I shut the door behind us. "So do you believe him?" I asked my brother.

"I don't know," Frank admitted. "But I think we need to find out if he's telling the truth. He's on our suspect list. If he's a liar, we need to know it."

"So we need to check out the dean's answering machine," I said.

"Yeah, and before the dean or his secretary get to the message—if there is one—and erase it," Frank added.

"So, tonight. After dinner?" I asked.

"Let's just hope no one absolutely needs to be served their potato chips specifically by us," Frank said. "It wouldn't—"

He was interrupted by a tap on the door.

"It's open," I called. I wondered if you earned the ability to lock your door when you became a master. I hadn't noticed.

David entered, carrying his backpack. He opened it and pulled out an oversize shoebox. The drawing of a lasso on the outside made me think it had once held cowboy boots. "Here you are." He dumped the box on my bed. "Now we're even. You saved my life. But if Liam finds out I took that, I'm totally dead."

"We'll get it back to you fast," Frank promised him.

"Put it in a bag or something," David instructed. "Don't go walking around the halls with it in sight."

"Got it," I said. David hurried out of the room.

I opened the lid of the shoebox and gave a low whistle.

"What?" Frank asked. He came over and sat on the end of my bed. I held up the lid so he could see the words "my Emma" printed over and over and over. In tiny letters. Filling up almost every speck of blank cardboard.

The words covered the inside of the box too, what I could see of it. Which wasn't much. The box was crammed full of . . . stuff. "Do you think he has the order memorized?" I asked.

"If there's an order to that, I don't see it," Frank said.

"Okay, then." I upended the box quickly, so the

contents landed in a pile on my bed. "If we look at stuff from the top of the pile down, and replace things in the box as we go, then the contents will be basically in the same place."

Frank picked up two movie stubs and glanced at them. "He must really like her. They went to that Sarah Jessica Parker chick flick." He put the stubs in the bottom of the box.

I flipped through the program that was next in the stack. "He went to see her in a synchronized swimming show."

"Twice," Frank said, pointing to an identical program deeper in the pile.

"I guess watching your girlfriend in a bathing suit for a couple of hours isn't such a hardship," I commented. "It's not like it was opera or anything." I returned the program to the box.

"Do you think Emma knows he has all this stuff?" Frank held up a sparkly hair thing shaped like a daisy. "Because if he just snags things like this without telling her, it's creepy."

"Very creepy," I agreed. I shook my head as I got to a chewed-up pencil. It was better than a chewed-up piece of gum. I guess.

"Now we're getting somewhere," Frank told me. "I just found a bio midterm of Emma's. She got a ninety-seven. I wonder if this could be the test Roy supposedly helped her cheat on."

"If it isn't, it doesn't seem like she'd need to cheat, does it?" I asked. "If you can get a ninety-seven on your own, you could help somebody else cheat."

Frank and I kept going through Liam's Emma collection. "Hey! Here's another copy of the test," I exclaimed.

"Not exactly," Frank said, looking over my shoulder. "I'm pretty sure the questions are in a different order. And look at the name on the top."

"Roy Duffy," I read.

"Looks like Ms. Campisi used to teach at Eagle River and teaches at the girls' school now," Frank told me.

Yep. Ms. Campisi's name was written in the lower left-hand corner of both tests. But the name of the school below her name was different on each test. Eagle River for Roy's. The Emerson School for Emma's.

"Guess she didn't feel like making up new tests," I commented.

"Guess she figured being at a new school and all, she didn't have to," Frank answered.

"There's no way to really prove that Emma saw

Roy's test before she took her midterm," I said. "Even if he showed Emma's dean both tests, it's not exactly hard evidence."

"But if Roy was willing to confess, that's a different story," Frank suggested. "If Roy told Emma that he had the two tests and that he was going to tell everything, that might be enough to freak her out."

"The fact that Liam has the tests doesn't look good for him. It supports the idea that Liam helped Emma take out Roy," I said. "At least it shows that Liam knew about the cheating . . . and probably the blackmail."

"One suspect. Two motives." Frank shook his head. "Either he wanted to help Emma out of the blackmail situation, so he killed Roy..."

"Or he was so obsessed with having Emma as his girlfriend that he killed Roy," I added.

"Or, of course, he didn't kill Roy at all," Frank reminded me as we continued to sort through the mementos. "Motives by themselves don't mean anything."

"Still, two motives for the same murder," I said as I put the last item back in the box. "That's not too shabby."

After dinner, without even taking the time to change into the socks with stars on them the servants had to wear at night, Frank and I headed across campus to the administration building.

It was time to find out if Mr. Diehl was actually Mr. Liar Liar Pants on Fire.

"Hold up," Frank said. "Security guard at four o'clock."

We stood motionless until he disappeared into the building next door to the one we had our eye on.

"Okay, let's get in there while we have a chance." Frank started across the lawn to the administration building, keeping low. I followed him. He tried the front door.

"Locked," he told me. "Not that that's a huge surprise."

We circled around the building. The other doors were locked too. And the windows on the first floor were closed tight. There was one window somebody had forgotten to close on the top floor.

But that was five stories up.

"That side door on the east is probably the fastest to pick," I said. "The problem is our friend, the security guard."

"Who might have friends of his own," Frank agreed. "But that gives me an idea. Do you have any gum?"

I pulled a pack from my pocket. He took the last four pieces and started chewing.

"Are you going to start oinking in a minute?" I asked. "You could have left me a piece."

"Here comes the guard. Come on," Frank said.

Then he rushed straight toward the guy.

"Hi," Frank said, just as the security guard stepped into the doorway of the administration building. "Can you help us? We're exchange students. We got a tour and everything. But this place is a lot bigger than our school. Where is the library again?"

"It *is* big," the guard agreed with a smile. Then he gave us incredibly easy-to-follow directions to the library.

Frank still managed to come up with a couple of questions to ask him. Then he gave me a kick, and I realized that I was supposed to be asking questions too. The guy probably thought we were exchange students from the Dummy Academy by the time we were finished.

"Thanks," Frank told the guard. Then we headed off in the direction of the library.

"What was that?" I asked Frank.

Frank grinned at me. "You'll see. Think he's moved on to the next building?"

I glanced over my shoulder. The security guard had disappeared. "Looks like he's gone," I answered.

"Then come on." Frank turned around and

dashed back to the administration building, up to the doorway where we'd just had our chat with the security guard. Frank grabbed the doorknob, pulled—and the door opened.

"How?" I wanted to know.

Frank pointed to the wad of freshly chewed gum he'd stuck in the lock. "Oink," he said.

"I didn't even see you do that," I told him.

"I'm just that good, little brother," Frank answered as we hurried to the dean's office. We'd been there the day we arrived.

"I guess we'll have to pick this one," I said when we reached the dean's door.

Frank reached out and twisted the knob. The door swung open. "Never hurts to try."

I stepped into the dim room and went right to the secretary's desk in the outer office. I checked the phone. "Message light's blinking," I told him.

"Let's see what we got," Frank answered.

I hit the retrieve messages button, and Frank and I listened as the dean's wife left a message at 5:43 asking the dean to stop on the way home and get dog food. That was it.

"We talked to Diehl at about ten after six," I said. "He told us he'd just left a message. A message from quarter to five is still on the machine. His should definitely be there."

Frank's eyes narrowed. "So he was lying. I wonder what else he's been lying about."

"Like what happened to Roy?" I asked.

"Diehl acts all concerned about the hazing. But he won't really do anything about it. Not even talk to the dean," Frank answered. "If he knew hazing had something to do with Roy's death, I don't know if he would have told the truth."

"Maybe it's that thing about hazing being this long academy tradition," I suggested. "He told us the administration expects the teachers to ignore it. Maybe he thought he'd get in trouble if he told the dean about the guys hazing David."

Frank looked over at the phone, thinking. "Maybe," he said finally. "And maybe he's covering up something about Roy's death for the same reason. All we know for sure is that he lied to us tonight. Let's get out of here."

Why had Diehl really lied? What about Liam's two motives? And what about Keith? He was so into the punishment thing. And Wes seemed to find the whole servant thing a complete good time. Then there was Douglas, with the daddy issues. Could he have pushed Roy way too hard just to make his father proud? And what about Emma? Was she freaked enough by Roy's blackmail to want to kill him?

All these questions kept spinning through my head as we walked back to the dorm. They were still spinning when I went to bed and tried to fall asleep.

Diehl had lied—but that didn't mean he was hiding anything about Roy's death. But somebody was. I could feel it. Roy hadn't had a heart attack while lying in his bed.

12.

Sinking

Somebody sat down on my bed. I opened my eyes. It was Roy Duffy.

Dead Roy Duffy.

I could see a little bit of the glue holding his eyelids shut. And even through the covers, I could feel the cold radiating off his body.

"So have you figured out who did it yet?" Roy asked, staring right at me, even though his eyes were permanently closed. "Who killed me?"

I struggled to sit up—a little freaked out, but curious. "So you were definitely killed? You didn't just have a heart attack?"

"I had a heart attack. But someone also killed me," Roy answered. "Want to see something cool?"

He unbuttoned his white dress shirt. I could see the rows of neat stitches that closed up his autopsy incisions. Roy ripped the incisions open. Like his flesh was just another shirt to pull aside.

I stared into the gaping hole in Roy's chest. "You aren't going to tell anything by just looking. You have to get dirty." He grabbed me by the wrists. His fingers were so cold they burned. Then he shoved my hands into his chest cavity, pressing them right up against his unbeating heart.

I recoiled. I tried to jerk away from Roy. But he wouldn't let go. "You're not really here," I yelled. "This is just a dream. It's a dream, and I'm waking up now."

I forced my eyes open. Roy was gone.

But there were still hands grasping my wrists. And a second later, my eyes were forced shut again as someone else wrapped a blindfold over them. My hands were pulled behind me and tied together. And I was gagged. At least the cloth of the gag tasted clean.

Then I was being marched out of my room and down the stairs. Again. Joe, too. At least I was pretty sure. I thought I'd heard him give a muffled protest.

I was sure we were in for another night in the cellar. But we went down only one flight of stairs, not two. And after some maneuvering, I was pushed outside. The crisp, cold air was nothing like the dankness of the basement.

"Watch your head," somebody ordered. Keith, I think. Then somebody was pressing down on my head, guiding me into a car. I concentrated on keeping track of the right and left turns as I was driven . . . somewhere. I thought there was a chance Joe and I could end up walking back.

I tried to figure out how many guys were in the car. It was hard to tell. No one was talking. But I was thinking maybe four or five besides me and Joe. I figured there were at least two in front. And I could hear two breathing from the seat behind me. I was almost positive Joe was next to me.

After three left turns and two right, the car came to a stop on what sounded like a gravel road. When the car door on my side was pulled open, I confirmed that the road was gravel by falling—or being shoved—out of the car and onto my knees. It was hard not to face-plant with my hands tied behind my back, but I managed to keep my balance.

Then somebody was pulling me up by my elbows and marching me off the gravel and onto what felt like dirt, or maybe even sand. "Step up!" one of the guys instructed. I picked up my foot and hit the side of something hard. "Higher!" the guy barked. I lifted my foot higher and stumbled into what I though was a boat.

Yeah. Definitely a boat. One of the guys helped me sit down on a wooden bench, and I could feel the shift from land to water. I could hear the slap of the oars. What did the guys have planned?

That question hammered in my brain as the boat traveled farther out into the water. What were they planning to do? If I could figure it out, *I* could make a plan. But I was clueless.

"This is good," someone said. Liam? I thought so.

Then someone had my shoulders. Someone had my feet. I was in the air. Swinging out.

Splash! I hit the water. For a moment I went straight down. I was too shocked to move.

Then I started to swim. Automatically, I tried to stroke with my arms, completely forgetting they were tied behind me. At least my legs were free. I managed to kick my way up to the surface.

I pulled in a deep breath through my nose. My mouth was still filled with the sodden gag. My blindfold was still on. How was I supposed to find my way out of the lake?

Stay calm, I ordered myself. That was the most important thing. I had to stay calm. That way, I could stay logical.

So where is the shore? I asked myself as I treaded

water. I heard some laughter over to the left. That had to be the guys in the boat. I heard some splashing on my right. Joe? Or water lapping against the shore?

I decided to assume it was shore. I listened for a few more seconds, then started to swim in that direction. Submerged again, it was like almost all my senses had been shut off. My vision had been gone to start with. But underwater, I couldn't hear. I couldn't smell.

All I had left was touch. I could feel the cold water against every inch of my skin. But the longer I stayed in the water, the less I could feel it. My body was getting numb. I had to get out of the lake.

Shouldn't I have reached shore by now?

"Frank, you're getting colder," I heard one of the guys shout.

So I'd been swimming in the wrong direction.

If I could trust the guys. As in, if I could trust the guys who had thrown me in the lake in the first place.

"You're getting warmer, Joe!" somebody yelled.

I decided to trust them. I didn't really think they'd want me to drown out here.

I turned around and started swimming in the opposite direction. It was hard to stay on any kind of course without being able to use my arms. It was hard to breathe, too. There was no smooth way to keep pulling myself out of the water for air. Every time I managed to suck in a breath through my nose, I felt like I was taking in as much H_2O as O_2.

The muscles in my legs started to burn from the extra work they were being forced to do. The fiery pain actually felt kind of good, because the rest of my body felt dead. So numb, it was like it almost didn't exist anymore.

Had the guys ever heard of hypothermia?

It wasn't the time to be thinking about that. It was the time to be swimming. So that's what I did—until I was sure I would have hit the shore if I'd been going in the right direction.

I treaded water again, my legs cramping in protest. I thought I heard someone shout "warmer." But was that warmer for me—or for Joe?

Maybe I'd just underestimated how far away the shore was. I didn't want to turn around if I was only feet away. I forced myself to return to swimming.

The cramp in my right leg intensified. It felt like a metal claw was ripping at the muscles and tendons. I tried to use my left leg to surface.

But my left leg was suddenly shredded with pain too. I couldn't kick.

I was going down.

Sinking down.

I struggled against the rope holding my wrists together. Too tight to break.

I kept sinking.

I needed air. I had to have air.

I kept sinking . . .

down . . .

down.

JOE

13.

Is He Breathing?

"Hot. You're getting very hot, Joe!" someone yelled.

The voice sounded close. So close.

But I didn't know if I could reach it. All the muscles felt like they'd been extracted from my legs. I was trying to swim with only long gobs of goo to propel me.

Stop your whining and kick, I ordered myself. *Or you're going to drown out here.* The thought got me swimming as hard as I could—with my hands tied behind me.

Then the toes on one foot hit something soft. The bottom of the lake! I really was almost to shore.

I stumbled to my feet and staggered the rest of the

way in. Then I collapsed onto the wet sand. My lungs felt like they'd been flattened into pancakes. As hard as I sucked in air, they just wouldn't inflate.

Someone gave me a kick in the side. Not that hard, but more than enough for a guy who was having trouble breathing because his lungs were pancakes.

"You going to try to steal another guy's girlfriend again?" a boy demanded.

"What?" I asked. It came out "whaaa?" because of the gag in my mouth.

"I said, are you going to try to steal another guy's girlfriend again?" the same boy—Liam, it had to be—asked again as I was rolled onto my back and my gag was ripped free. My blindfold was torn off a second later.

Yeah, it was Liam doing the interrogating. He was crouching over me, practically snarling.

"Where's Frank?" I asked. I managed to sit up. I didn't see my brother anywhere.

"Answer the question!" Liam yelled.

"I never tried to steal anyone's girlfriend in the first place. So no, I won't be doing it again," I shot back. "Now, where's my brother?"

"I don't see Frank," Douglas said. He sounded panicked.

"He's out there," Liam answered. "He's just afraid to come in."

"He's still in the water?" I burst out. "Are you insane? I almost drowned out there. You have to let me go find him!"

"Come on, Liam. You know these guys were only talking to Emma. Let Joe go get Frank," Keith said. "This is getting out of control."

"It's true. We talked to her for less than a minute. And that's all we did—talked. Right out in front of everyone." I scrambled unsteadily to my feet. "I'm going back out there. Are you going to untie my hands before I do, or not?"

Liam stared at me for a few seconds, then roughly untied my wrists. "Go. Just remember, you'll get a lot worse if I see you near Emma again."

I scanned the dark lake. The surface was smooth. I didn't see Frank anywhere out there.

"He was getting close to shore when you climbed out," Douglas told me. "I thought he'd be right behind you."

I plunged into the water. "Frank!" I shouted.

He didn't answer.

I dived under. I couldn't see that much more clearly than when I'd had the blindfold on. Where was he?

I turned my head slowly back and forth, trying to divide the lake bottom into quadrants so that I'd be sure not to miss anything.

My lungs were already screaming out for oxygen. I didn't care, though. I wasn't letting myself surface until I found Frank.

Wait. Over there. Was that a shadow? Or—

I swam closer. My stomach heaved as the shadow turned into my brother. Lying on the bottom of the lake. Completely still.

I shoved my hands under his armpits and scissored my legs until we both broke the surface. "Help!" I shouted. "Help me get him in!"

I adjusted my grip so I had one arm under Frank's chin, keeping his head above water. Then I began to tow him to shore.

All three guys—Douglas, Keith, and Liam—charged out into the lake to meet me. Douglas and Liam grabbed Frank. Keith helped me back onto the beach. "Is Frank okay?" I cried out.

I couldn't see his chest rising and falling. He lay on the sand, motionless.

"Is he breathing?" I shouted.

Silence.

FRANK

14.

Don't Die on Me

"Don't die on me," someone mumbled, close to my ear. "Don't die on me."

What? Why?

My thoughts felt like they were moving through Jell-O, instead of my brain. I just couldn't *focus*.

"I am not having someone else die on me."

Hands pressed down on my chest. Hard. As that same voice counted out, "One, two, three, four, five."

I coughed, and I tasted the lake as what felt like half of it came pouring out of my mouth.

"Turn him on his side!" a new voice yelled.

And hands immediately rolled me off my back.

The lake water continued to spew out of me. Then, finally, I was able to draw a breath. A shallow, shaky breath followed up by more coughing.

"You could have killed him!" I heard Joe shout.

"I'm okay," I managed to say.

"No thanks to these cretins," Joe burst out. "They almost killed both of us. Just because we *talked* to Liam's girlfriend."

"What?" I asked. I sat up—and the whole beach spun around underneath me.

"Let's not stand around talking about it. We need to get them back," Douglas said. He threw a pair of Eagle River sweats at me. "You should put these on. You're soaked."

Like it was something that had just weirdly happened to me. Like he and his friends hadn't blindfolded me, gagged me, tied my hands together and thrown me into a lake.

But I wasn't going to turn down dry clothes. I pulled off my pajamas and got into the sweats as fast as I could. Which still wasn't fast enough to stop my whole body from breaking out in goose bumps.

"Let's get back. This isn't fun anymore," Keith said.

I wondered when it had stopped being a gigglefest for him. For me, I think it was when I felt myself sinking, and my legs were too weak to get me back to the surface.

Joe rushed over and stuck out his hand. "You really okay?" he asked as he pulled me to my feet.

"Yeah. You? Looks like you went swimming too." Joe had on Eagle River sweats, and his wet hair was plastered to his head.

"I'm all right," he told me. But he looked wrung out, and I noticed his legs shaking as we climbed into the car.

The trip back to the dorm was silent. Joe was halfway falling asleep, and the other guys seemed shell-shocked.

All I wanted was to fall back into bed. But once I finally got there, I couldn't get my brain to shut off. It felt like it was working more slowly. But it was working. There was something Liam had said when he was doing CPR on me. Something important. But I just couldn't bring it back.

"You missed a fine performance from our friend Liam tonight—when you were drowning," Joe said.

"Yeah?"

"Oh, yeah. He had a full-on psycho episode. The whole reason we got tossed in the lake was because Liam thought we were trying to steal his girlfriend. Even though, *hello*, if I was going to try to date anyone it would have been that girl Lil. She was way cool. I usually like long hair on girls, but I liked short on her. It made her look like an elf. In a good way."

"You're kind of babbling," I said.

"Yeah. Near-death experiences kind of do that to me, I guess," Joe answered. "Suddenly I feel like I'm completely revved up. Maybe I just have way too much adrenaline left and nothing to do with it. Like swim, or scream for help."

"What did Liam say to you? He said something to me that I'm trying to remember," I told Joe.

"Make that what did he *scream*—with spit flying out of his mouth," Joe corrected. "He just kept asking me if I was done trying to steal other guys' girlfriends. And he told me that he didn't want to ever see me near Emma again. Is that what he said to you?"

I shook my head—then I immediately wished I hadn't. The last thing my brain needed was to be sloshed around.

"He was giving me CPR," I said slowly, trying to remember. I closed my eyes, trying to get back to the moment. "And he was telling me not to die on him." My eyes snapped open. "He said he wasn't going to have *someone else* die on him."

"So he killed Roy," Joe exclaimed. "I didn't think

Liam was the kind of guy who could kill someone. Not until tonight. The way he just had me do one push-up that time made me think he was really laid-back and everything. But tonight he was like a completely different person."

There was something in all those words of Joe's that didn't quite make sense. I took a minute to sort it out. "I don't think we can definitely say that Liam killed Roy. Maybe Liam was just in the room when Roy died. Maybe he tried to save Roy."

"Save him after he almost killed him? The way he did you?" Joe asked.

"I don't know," I admitted.

"You know what we need to do? We need to check out that notebook of Mr. Diehl's again. See what it says about the night Roy died," Joe said.

"Good idea." I struggled to my feet.

"We don't have to do it tonight. You look pretty wiped." Joe reached out a hand to steady me.

"It's only one flight up," I answered. "And Diehl's almost definitely asleep. It's the perfect time."

I hate to admit it, but I was kind of out of breath by the time we climbed the stairs and walked down the hall to Mr. Diehl's office. I let Joe open the door. My hands were a little shaky for the job.

A couple of twists with a straightened-out paper

clip we found on the floor, and we were in. That's what ATAC training will do for you.

The notebook wasn't on Diehl's desk anymore, but it didn't take us long to find it. Third drawer down, under the World History text and a box of Kleenex. "February thirteenth, February thirteenth," Joe muttered as he flipped through the pages. "Here we go. This is Diehl's entry for the night Roy died."

"Read it to me," I requested.

"Here goes," Joe said. "'Wednesday. The masters take one of the boys down to the cellar alone for a private session.'"

"So the boy is Roy." I could feel my heart starting to beat faster. We were about to find out the truth of what happened the night Roy died.

"'They circle around him. He's shaking. He's terrified. He reaches for the knife he has strapped to his leg,'" Joe continued to read.

"Whoa. Roy brought a knife down to the cellar?" I exclaimed.

"I know. That's hard-core," Joe said. He started to read again. "'But the knife slips from his fingers. All the masters see it fall to the ground. The servant tries to grab it but he's too slow. One of the masters grabs it, and slashes at the servant with it.'"

"No way!"

"Yeah, I know. Listen to the rest," Joe answered. " 'The servant brings up his hands to try to protect his face. The knife cuts into one hand. Slash. Slash. The servant backs up, lowering his hand. The master advances and uses the knife to slice the servant's face. Once. Twice.' "

"No way!" I said again. I couldn't believe what I was hearing.

" 'Then the masters leave the servant there. Bleeding onto the cellar floor.' " Joe looked up at me. "That's it for the thirteenth."

"Except that's not what happened to Roy," I protested. "Not even close. Roy didn't have any cuts on his body. ATAC would have told us if he did. And there wasn't any mention of a heart attack. Are you sure you're looking at February thirteenth?"

Joe flipped back a page. "Yep. February thirteenth."

I spotted a calendar on Mr. Diehl's wall. I flipped back to February. "The thirteenth wasn't even on a Wednesday this year."

"Maybe the notebook isn't about this year's hazing." Joe turned to the first page. "I don't see a year anywhere. The entries just have the month and day."

"We could use Zeller's Rule to figure out what

years February thirteenth fell on a Wednesday," I said.

"Huh?"

"No, wait. For Zeller's you have to already know the year. It tells you the day of the week if you know the year and the date," I corrected.

"Again I say, huh?" Joe said.

"It's a formula where *k* is—"

"Never mind. I bet I know what year the notebook is about. And without any Zelber's whatever," Joe told me. "Mr. Diehl went here. He told us that, remember?"

"Yeah. And the scars on his face definitely match the injuries the servant got," I said.

"That's really sick. I feel sorry for the guy," Joe answered. "But the notebook's not going to give us any answers about what happened to Roy."

15.

Judgment Day

I couldn't stop staring at Mr. Diehl during history the next day. Staring at the scars on his face and hands. How could he stand to teach here after what had happened to him as a first-year student?

As for Liam, no doodling for him today. He spent most of his time shooting fast little looks at me. Making sure I was still breathing? After what he, Keith, and Douglas did?

By the time the bell rang, I'd only managed to add two sentences about Mr. Diehl's lecture to my notebook. All that staring and being stared at had given me the willies. Plus, I kept thinking about the investigation. I needed to get back to the dorm, where Frank and I could figure out our next step.

But before I'd made it halfway there, someone grabbed my arm.

Which felt like it had been happening every few seconds lately.

I found myself being tugged behind a clump of trees along the path. And you won't believe who'd done the tugging. I didn't. It was Emma Whitley. As in, the girl I was never supposed to get near again.

I pulled my arm out of her grip. "You could have just tried something like, 'I need to speak to you. Would you step over here for a minute.' Anything along those lines," I told her.

"Shut up," she answered. Clearly, she had all kinds of politeness issues. "If Liam sees me talking to you, he's not going to be happy."

"And an unhappy Liam is . . . pretty much a psycho killer," I answered.

"That's what I wanted to talk to you about." Emma stepped deeper into the stretch of trees. "Would you please come over here so that no one will see us?"

I moved over to her. I didn't want anyone to see us either. And she had asked, instead of just grabbing.

"I heard what Liam did to you and your brother last night," Emma told me. "Liam called me after it happened. He was totally freaked. I think he might actually have been crying."

"Poor, poor Liam," I said. "My brother was at the bottom of the lake. He'd stopped breathing."

"I know." Emma shoved her hands through her long hair. "I know, I know, I know. And that is so horrible. It's just that Liam . . . he gets so incredibly jealous. He just loses it sometimes."

"And that's okay with you? You're okay with having a boyfriend who *loses it* like that?" I asked. "Aren't you even a little bit afraid that you'll be facing some Liam rage yourself someday? Even if you don't care about anyone else."

Emma's eyes widened. "I *do* care. Of course I care." She pulled a leaf off one of the trees and twisted it in her fingers. "It's just that I . . . I really love him, you know? And most of the time, he's great. He's funny. And sweet. He just has to get control of this jealousy thing. I keep trying to convince him that he has nothing to be jealous of. But he just won't get it."

She dropped the mangled leaf. "So you and your brother, you're both all right?"

"Yeah. But what about Roy?"

Emma's mouth dropped open, and she didn't say anything for a second. Then she asked, "Roy? What about Roy?"

"Do you think Liam could have killed Roy? Maybe not on purpose, but do you think he could have forced him to, like, do push-ups for so many hours that Roy had a heart attack?"

Emma's face paled. Fast. As fast as water pours out of an upended glass. "I always thought there was something weird about Roy's death," she admitted. "No one outside of the academy is supposed to know what goes on between the servants and the masters, but a lot of the girls at my school do. I do, because Roy and Liam both told me stuff. Roy was having a really hard time."

"So, are you saying you think Liam could have accidentally killed Roy?" I asked, careful to keep my voice low and calm.

"No!" Emma exclaimed. "No, Roy and I were a couple when he died. Liam couldn't have been jealous. I wasn't even his girlfriend then." She sucked in a deep breath. "I think something bad might have happened, though. Some out-of-control hazing thing."

"You know, a guy doesn't have to be with a girl to be jealous," I said. I know, I know. It's not like I've had all that much experience in this area. But it's not exactly rocket science. "A guy can be jealous of someone's boyfriend, if the guy wants to be with the girl himself."

Emma didn't have anything to say to that.

"Do you think Liam could have sort of had his eye on you when you were going out with Roy? Do you think he could have wanted Roy out of the way?" I asked.

"If he did, he never said anything to me. I never got any vibe from Liam," Emma answered. "Not that I was paying that much attention. 'Cause I was going out with Roy."

"So Roy was a good boyfriend?" I asked. I hated to do it. I knew I could be hurting her if she really had cared about Roy. But I wanted to see her reaction—because Emma was a suspect too.

Emma yanked another leaf off a tree and started twisting. "Roy—" She snapped her mouth shut. "I think I hear someone coming. I have to get out of here. Tell your brother I'm glad he's okay. Tell him Liam is really, really sorry."

Then she bolted.

I bolted too. I wanted to find Frank and get him up to speed. I found him in the lobby of the dorm, checking our mail slot.

"Aunt Trudy sent cookies," he told me.

"Excellent," I said. I lowered my voice. "Emma Whitley gave me a message for you."

"You talked to her? Are you insane?" Frank burst out.

"She started it," I answered. "She grabbed me." I looked around to make sure no one was close enough to overhear us. "She wanted us to know that Liam is really sorry. That he almost cried—that's how sorry he was. He just has these jealousy management problems. And so the upshot is that, basically, we should forgive him."

Frank rolled his eyes. "Were you able to talk to her about Roy at all?"

"Tried," I answered. "She practically sprinted away as soon as I started trying to find out if he was a good boyfriend or not. But she says there's no way Liam went all jealous on Roy and gave him a heart attack. She says Liam wouldn't have been jealous of Roy, because Liam wasn't her boyfriend when she was with Roy."

Frank rolled his eyes again. "Did you tell her that you get jealous when M.J. kisses Spider-Man?"

"No. Because that's not true," I answered.

Frank laughed. See, he totally has no sense of humor. He doesn't laugh when things are funny. He laughs when they aren't.

I ignored him. "The weird thing is that when she was talking to me about what a great guy he was, for a minute I could see it. That first day I met him, when he made me do a push-up for not knowing all—or most of—the lyrics to 'Bohemian Rhapsody,' he seemed cool. And his favorite song is 'Bohemian Rhapsody.' How bad can you be and have that as your favorite song?"

"Bad enough to almost drown both of us," Frank reminded me.

"Oh. Right. That. Okay, so he's at the top of the suspect list," I said.

"It's not like he did it alone, though," Frank answered. "He was definitely the leader last night. But Keith and Douglas were with him."

"So what do you think we do now?" I asked.

"I'm thinking we hit the servant lounge with these." He gave Aunt Trudy's box of cookies a shake. "The servants knew all the masters, and they knew Roy. There's got to be some info we can get out of them."

"And we have to sacrifice the baked goods to do it?" I complained as we started up the stairs.

" 'Fraid so," Frank said. "No one said this job would be easy."

But he opened the box and held it out to me. I grabbed three of Aunt Trudy's famous cookies—pretty much everything tasty in one place. Caramel, chocolate chips, nuts, coconut. I concentrated on enjoying every bite. I doubted there would be any more cookies when we left the lounge.

“I want to toss my backpack in our room,” Frank said.

“Sounds good.”

He opened the door.

And the bite of cookie I had in my mouth went down the wrong way. For a second I couldn’t breathe.

Our room was filled with people.

And no, it wasn’t a surprise party. At least not the good kind.

Every guy in the room was a master. That was clear from the long black robes they all wore.

“Put this on,” one of the guys said. I couldn’t tell who. They all had their hoods on. He tossed white robes to me and Frank.

“We’re taking you down to the cellar.”

What were we supposed to do? We were severely outnumbered.

So we let ourselves be herded down, down, down. Into the darkness of the cellar. Where, as you might recall, no one can hear you scream.

And I wanted to scream. I admit it. After last night, I wanted to scream the place down. Of course, I didn’t.

I stood silently in the center of the cellar. Surrounded by black-robed figures.

Finally, The Voice began to speak. Now I knew

it was just a regular guy with a voice disguiser strapped over his throat. But it was still creepy.

"We have been informed of the events of last night," The Voice boomed. "And we will not tolerate them."

What? Was The Voice mad that we'd almost drowned? Were Frank and I too bad at swimming to be considered as servants? I didn't get it.

The boy directly in front of me—who I was pretty sure was operating The Voice—lifted his arms. "Bring them to us."

Huh? Because Frank and I were about three feet away from the guy.

In a second it became clear that the "us" wasn't me and Frank. It was Douglas, Keith, and Liam. They were brought into the circle with me and Frank. They had their black robes on, but the hoods were down, making it easy to see their faces. And their hands were tied behind them.

I didn't get it.

"These masters are in shame," The Voice explained. "Their actions last night were not sanctioned by the group. They acted on their own. They have shamed us all."

Douglas looked ready to puke. I would bet money he was thinking about his dad. About how his dad would react to knowing he had done something that the masters—all those future business contacts—hated so much.

Keith looked mad. Like he couldn't believe the masters were daring to say this to him.

And Liam just looked wrung out. He had dark circles under his eyes, as if he hadn't slept for a year.

"It is our duty today to determine the fate of our shamed brothers," The Voice went on. Wes, I realized. Wes was the voice. I recognized the tips of his red Converse sneakers.

"Frank Hardy. Joe Hardy. You are not yet masters. But you were the victims of these three masters' crimes," Wes pronounced. "You must determine their punishment. Whatever you decide is fair will be done without question."

16.

It's Happening Again

I glanced at Joe. What were we supposed to do here? If we didn't ask for any punishment, it would look suspicious. Like maybe we were planning to go to the school administrators—or even the cops.

But I definitely didn't want to ask for anything that could go down dangerous, like swimming blindfolded, gagged, with tied-up hands.

"The blood?" Joe asked me.

"Yeah," I agreed. I turned toward the masters. "We think they should each drink some of that blood you gave us the first night."

"A lot. A whole glass," Joe added.

That actually *was* punishment. The stuff was

disgusting. I felt like my stomach needed washing after I drank that one sip.

"So be it," The Voice said. I realized The Voice was Wes. Those red sneakers gave him away. He flicked his hand, and one of the masters rushed away and up the cellar stairs.

Then we all waited for him to come back. Waited and waited and waited. *What's the recipe for the 'blood,'* I wondered. *Does it involve hanging out until chickens lay rotten eggs, or what?*

Finally, the master who'd left returned with a tray holding three of the beaten-up metal chalices. "Sorry," he muttered. "Diehl had snagged the blender, as usual, and I had to get it back. It had all this gunk in the bottom, as usual. But I didn't bother to clean it out. More gunk, better blood. Am I right?"

"Do you have any understanding of the phrase 'too much information'?" Wes asked. The question sounded ridiculous in the booming Voice of Doom.

The master with the tray shrugged. "Just thought you'd want to know where I was."

Wes picked up one of the chalices. He pressed it into Liam's hands. "Drink," he ordered. The Voice sounded a lot better when issuing commands. It didn't make me feel like giggling.

"And chug it," one of the other masters ordered.

"I want to see you suck it all down at once."

"No spitting out," someone else added. "You spit it out, you lick it up."

Liam nodded, his face serious. Then he swallowed the blood, his throat muscles working as he drank and drank. He grimaced as he finished and wiped his mouth with his arm. "That doesn't seem like enough. Not after what we did."

"Shut up," Keith told him. "That whole thing was your idea."

"Yeah, I didn't want to—," Douglas began.

"You shut up too," Keith snapped at Douglas. "You'd be afraid to take a breath on your own if you weren't more afraid of Daddy."

"I just meant that we almost killed those guys. Drinking a glass of nasty isn't exactly—"

Liam's body began to convulse.

His eyes opened so wide I could see a ring of white all the way around them.

Then he collapsed, continuing to spasm.

"It's happening again!" someone yelled.

"It's just like Roy," someone else shouted. "Look at him!"

Liam's body was shuddering. He was staring up at us, but I didn't think he was seeing anything at all.

Wes threw off his hood and ripped the voice

modifier off his throat. "This time, we have to get help."

"No!" Douglas shoved his hood back. "We can't. We'll all get suspended. We can deal with this. Someone just start CPR."

"Liam is the one who knows it."

Joe and I knew CPR too. But I thought Liam needed more help than we could give him. I whirled around and pounded for the stairs.

"Stop him!" Douglas shouted. "If he gets away, we're all getting kicked out of school. Or worse. We could all go to jail."

I felt someone grab the back of my robe.

"I got this one, Frank," Joe cried.

A second later I heard the sound of a body hitting the ground, accompanied by a surprised "Ooof."

"Thanks," I called.

"No problem," Joe answered.

I was at the stairs now. Taking them three at a time.

I could hear people coming after me, but I didn't look back.

17.

Poisoned

Another one of the masters charged at Frank. I was not letting anyone get past me. Liam could die if Frank didn't get help.

I lowered my shoulder, aimed at the part of the robe where I figured the knees hit, and hurled myself forward. The master went down, and so did I.

I shoved myself to my feet. Four other masters were moving toward the stairs. Frank was about halfway up them.

There were a lot of stairs.

"You don't get it," one of the masters yelled. "This comes out, it's no college for any of us. Maybe even jail."

I scanned the floor. I spotted a chunk of concrete that had broken off the stairs. I snagged it and held it up. "I'm the pitcher on my school's team. I can throw at eighty-seven miles an hour. Clocked."

Big lie. But lying is, like, a requirement of being an ATAC agent.

"So who wants a piece of this?" I called out.

That got a moment of hesitation from the masters. I backed up to the stairs and started to climb them, still facing down the masters. Still holding the chunk of concrete.

As I moved higher, I got a clear view of Liam down on the floor. His body had stopped jerking and heaving—but the stillness was even worse. Was the guy still alive?

A couple of the other boys were crouched near him. But they didn't seem to know how to help.

I reached the midpoint of the staircase, then turned and bolted. Immediately I heard footsteps as some of the masters chased after me. I reached the door first. I pushed through and slammed it behind me.

Now I just needed a way to keep it closed. It didn't lock from this side. They were going to be on me in a couple of seconds. Did Frank have time to get help?

I had no way of knowing. I just had to keep the

door shut. That was my only mission right now.

I checked the hall. Nothing big enough to jam against the door. There was no time to go find something.

Wait. I had it. It wouldn't keep the masters down there for long—but maybe for long enough. I whipped off my white robe, then tied one end to the doorknob and the other end to the heating pipes. I stretched the cloth as tight as I could.

Then I took off. Frank might need me. I raced up the stairs to the first floor of the dorm. The TV lounge was empty—because all the masters were in the cellar. Frank had grabbed the phone that was behind the mail counter.

"There's a victim of nicotine poisoning at the Eagle River Academy. Royce Hall. The cellar," Frank said into the phone, speaking slowly and clearly.

Nicotine poisoning? Where had my brother gotten that?

Did he think there had been poison in the fake blood? Liam's reaction to it made it likely. But why had Frank zeroed in on nicotine?

I knew ingesting nicotine could poison you. Probably give you convulsions. But lots of substances could do that.

"We have to get up to Diehl's office," Frank said as he hung up.

"Diehl? Do you think he'll actually do something this time? Wouldn't it be better to just wait for the EMTs so we get them down to the cellar ASAP?" I asked.

Frank didn't answer. He just took off, heading for the stairs.

I chased after him.

Then, as we tore up to Diehl's office, I got it. Nicotine poisoning. Nicotine, as in one of the ingredients in cigarettes. Frank and I had seen a pack of cigarettes on Diehl's desk. Plus, I suddenly remembered, the blender had been in Diehl's office. And there had been gunk in the bottom of it that hadn't been cleaned out before the master had mixed up the blood.

Frank slammed open the door to Diehl's office. Diehl jerked his head up from the papers he was grading.

"We need the first-aid kit," Frank barked.

Diehl leaped to his feet and pulled the kit down from the top of the filing cabinet. "What's happened?"

Frank ignored him. "Does the kit have concentrated charcoal?" he asked.

"Yes," Diehl said.

Frank grabbed the kit and handed it over to me. "Give some to Liam," he instructed.

I got back down to the cellar door in record time. It was open a couple of inches, and a few of the masters were shoving on it.

"Back off," I told them. "I have some medicine I need to get to Liam." I slammed the door shut and started working on the knots. Why'd I have to make them so tight in the first place?

I got one end free and shoved open the door. The masters on the stairs stepped back as I ran past them.

I knelt down next to Liam and pulled the concentrated charcoal out of the kit. I quickly read the instructions and got some of the stuff down Liam's throat.

"What does that do?" Keith asked.

"Is he going to be okay?" Douglas said. I had the feeling that Douglas was a lot more worried about himself.

"It should make him puke up the poison," I answered.

"What poison?" Wes cried. "Nobody gave anybody poison." He whipped his head toward the master who'd been sent to fetch the blood. "You just mixed it up like usual, right?"

"Yeah. Mayonnaise, Tabasco, those violet candies—"

"Help me roll him onto his side. We don't want him to suck back his own vomit," I said.

Douglas and Keith had Liam on his side before I could even touch him. Liam's body began to convulse again, his eyelids twitching. Then he let go a stream of red vomit. I had to remind myself it was only red because of all the food coloring in the phony blood.

"The EMTs are here," one of the guys called down the stairs.

"You called them?" Douglas exclaimed.

"You want Liam to die?" I shot back.

The EMTs got to work. Fast. Efficient.

But were they in time?

"Is he going to be okay?" I asked.

"He should be," one of the EMTs answered. "We'll do everything we can."

Nice.

FRANK

18.

Conspiracy of Silence

Joe and I watched Mr. Diehl walk out of the dorm, escorted by two police officers. His hands were cuffed behind his back. It made him look kind of like one of the servant boys. I guess that was just because we'd had our hands tied behind us so many times.

Mr. Diehl turned back to face us—and the other guys who'd gathered to watch the scene, along with Dean McCormack. "It will stop now!" Diehl shouted. "I'll talk to every reporter. They'll listen to me, even though no one at this school would. I tried for years until I gave up talking. But now I'll go on every news show that will have me. It will finally stop!"

Dean McCormack shook his head as the police

helped Diehl into the back of the car. "I never would have picked Geoffrey to be a killer. Never in a thousand years. He's always seemed the timid type."

"Poisoning someone isn't exactly brave," Joe said.

"You're right," the dean agreed.

We watched the cop car drive away in silence. When it was out of sight, Dean McCormack shook his head again. "I don't even know what he was talking about at the end. When he was saying it would finally stop. *What* will finally stop?"

I couldn't believe how clueless this man was. Even if he didn't know Mr. Diehl's personal history, he had to know that Liam had almost been killed down in the cellar in what any bozo could figure out was a hazing ritual.

"We found a notebook in Mr. Diehl's office," Joe began. "At first we thought it was a record he was keeping about hazing activity in the dorm."

I saw a couple of the guys exchange nervous looks.

"But it was about what happened to him and the other boys the year he was a servant, back when he was a student at the academy," Joe continued. "Those scars on his hands and face? He got those down in the cellar."

"Seriously?" Keith burst out.

"Seriously," Joe told him.

"We think Mr. Diehl was willing to kill a couple

of kids to stop hazing forever," I said. "Or maybe he didn't really think anyone would actually die. Maybe he thought the nicotine would just cause a convulsion, and that would be enough to show outsiders what was happening at the school. Because EMTs would have to be called."

Dean McCormack scrubbed his face with his fingers. "This is such a shock. I'm processing everything too slowly. You said Mr. Diehl was willing to kill a couple of kids. So you believe he's responsible for Roy Duffy's death, too?"

I nodded. "We think Roy got a dose of nicotine too. We think Mr. Diehl did it the same way he did tonight. Just unwrapped some cigarettes and dumped them in the bottom of the blender. Probably with some liquid to disguise them. The EMTs said the amount of nicotine in four cigarettes is enough to kill an adult."

"I know it's a powerful toxin," the dean said. "It's even used as a pesticide. With Roy's heart condition, he probably never had a chance of surviving."

"I don't think he did." Douglas stepped up to the dean. "I was there the night Roy died. He didn't have a heart attack in his bed. It happened down in the cellar. Almost the same way it did with Liam. We gave him some of this fake blood mixture we use on all the servants. But Roy . . ."

Douglas stopped and swallowed hard, then managed to go on. "With Roy . . . Nothing had ever happened like it did with Roy. We gave him some of the blood to drink. Then he started spasming."

"It was freaky," Keith said, joining Douglas in front of the dean. "I thought he was faking at first. Trying to scare us, the way we always try to scare the servants."

"Then he was dead. It happened so fast," Douglas explained. "Liam did CPR on him—he'd taken a class. But it was too late. Roy was gone."

"Why didn't you boys come to me?" Dean McCormack asked.

I really wanted to hear the answer to that one.

"Roy was dead," Keith said. "We couldn't bring him back."

"We knew if we told you, we'd get expelled," Wes added. "We all talked about it, and we decided since there wasn't anything we could do for Roy, we'd save ourselves. We put him in his bed and left him there."

"We all knew about his heart condition. There were some things he couldn't do in PE," Douglas continued. "We figured that everyone would think he just died of a heart attack. But if we could have done something to save him, we would have."

Would they? Some of them, maybe. But would

Douglas? He really didn't want me going to get help for Liam.

At least Douglas had stepped up now. He'd told the truth. About everything. And that had to count for something.

"The teens who took part in the hazing have been sentenced to sixty hours of community service each," the newscaster said.

Joe, Mom, Dad, Aunt Trudy, and I lounged in our living room. I can't tell you how psyched Joe was to have TV access again. Even if right now he was watching the news, instead of his beloved *Aqua Teen*. Like there is anything at all believable about a meatball and some fries solving crimes.

JOE

Joe here. Frank forgot to mention the shake. And that show rocks. Believable, shmelievable. Who cares? It's a cartoon, Frank! Okay, I'm out.

The newscaster switched over to a reporter who

was talking to Mr. Diehl. Diehl was in prison, waiting for his trial.

"I never meant for anyone to die," Mr. Diehl told the reporter. "What happened to Roy was tragic. But I couldn't let his death stop me from doing what had to be done to stop the hazing."

Mom shook her head. "I don't understand why he didn't just go to the police from the beginning."

"Diehl saw a kid almost have an asthma attack because he was forced to do jumping jacks with a gag in his mouth—and he said nothing," I answered. "It's like he had to make the fact that there was hazing come out without actually having a face-to-face confrontation with anyone."

"Wimp, wimp, wimp," Playback called from his living room perch.

"Exactly," Joe said. He stood up and wandered into the kitchen.

On the TV screen, the first newscaster was back, talking about how Mr. Diehl's case had prompted some talk of putting antihazing legislation on the books.

"I wonder if laws would help," I said. "The thing about hazing is that it's so secret. And it's gone on forever, so everyone acts like it's just part of going to school. This guy Douglas we met, his dad was one hundred percent behind the hazing."

"The laws are the place to start," Dad answered.

Joe came back into the room carrying a couple of bowls of tortilla chips and a bowl of salsa. He deposited them on the coffee table.

Aunt Trudy leaped to her feet. "What are you doing?" she exclaimed.

"Getting us some snacks," Joe said. "And I know we just ate dinner. And dinner was great. But now it's snack time."

"If snacks need to be gotten in this house, I'll do the getting," Aunt Trudy told us. "Those two boys on the exchange program—Jamie and Andrew—would never let me do a thing! They even made my bed. It was weird, I tell you. Especially the way they walked around looking at the floor all the time."

Joe plopped down on the floor and snagged a chip. "You want to serve me stuff, I have no problem with it," he said to Aunt Trudy. "In fact, I could use an orange soda."

Aunt Trudy made like she was going to get up—and then she plopped back down again. "Sorry, Joe—I hang up my servant hat after eight p.m."

Now that's what I'm talking about. It was good to be home.